April's Promise

Forever Love series, Book 1

Karen Rose Smith

Published by Karen Rose Smith
Copyright 2013 Karen Rose Smith

ISBN: 978-0-9890448-3-7

http://www.karenrosesmith.com
http://www.karenrosesmithmysteries.com

Chapter One

Gabe Chronister didn't know how one three-year-old little girl could cause so much havoc!

His nanny had left for a family emergency and he'd thought he could handle working from home and caring for Stephie at the same time. After all, he was a CEO. After all, he took care of his little girl every night after the nanny left.

This wasn't the same. This was twenty-four hours a day and much harder than running his business.

Unexpectedly, he thought about the times April had been here since Vanessa had died. She'd handled Stephie with an aplomb and ease he suspected his wife had never felt.

Two sisters who were opposites really. They'd been

raised with advantages yet April treated the advantages much differently than Vanessa had.

Just why was he comparing? Because he felt guilty April had always been a shadow in the back of his mind?

Stephie pounded her tiny fist on the table. From her position in her booster seat, she looked…

"More sketti!" she demanded like either a princess or a tyrant. She didn't look quite like either with pasta in her hair and tomato sauce smeared all over her face. Bath time tonight would be a battle.

Wasn't everything these days?

The phone rang.

This time Stephie pointed to the chocolate cookies he'd placed in the center of the table as incentive for her to eat spaghetti and a piece of broccoli first.

"Cookie?" she pleaded with one of those smiles that always melted his heart.

He reached for another forkful of spaghetti realizing he hadn't been quick enough with it. "Have some more of this first—"

The phone rang again. Putting down the fork, he stood and crossed to the counter, picking up the cordless phone. Checking caller ID, he saw the name and number. He considered letting the call go to voicemail, but he didn't. He answered.

"Hi, Winnifred," he greeted his mother-in-law who'd sold her house in Cedar Corners, Virginia, to move with a friend to a retirement village in Florida.

Stephie pointed to the cookies again and asked in a higher voice, "Cookies, please?"

How could he explain she needed to eat more than two spaghetti noodles before she could have a cookie?

Obviously hearing her granddaughter in the background, Winnifred asked, "Is this a bad time?"

"Just a busy time. Dinner for Stephie."

"And how about *you*?"

He might be warming up spaghetti around midnight. There were e-mails to return before he could think about eating.

"I'm fine," he told her, convincing himself he was.

"Daddee—daddee—daddee!" The last "daddee" was practically a wail and he was sure Winnifred heard it.

"Where's Evelyn?"

"Evelyn's daughter is pregnant with twins and now is confined to bed rest. She went to Pennsylvania to help her."

"And what are *you* going to do?"

All of a sudden Stephie began rocking back and

forth on her booster seat. He was afraid she'd fall off the chair.

"Winnifred, I've got to go." He started around the table to Stephie, ready to end the call.

"What are you going to do, Gabe?" his mother-in-law asked again.

Reaching Stephie, he answered tersely, "Find another nanny. Stephie, sit still," he ordered with as much authority as he'd use directing one of his employees.

His daughter began crying.

He thought he heard Winnifred murmur, "Good luck," as he glanced around at the state of his kitchen and exhaled a long, slow breath.

****

Gabe needs you.

April Remmington could hear her mother's voice as clearly as if Winnifred Remmington were standing beside her.

Waiting at her brother-in-law's door in the dimming light, April rang the bell a second time. As the October breeze tossed russet leaves around the pillars on the porch, she tried to lock the secret she carried in a tight box in her heart.

If Gabe ever found out what she knew—

After a few more minutes, she turned the knob and pushed the door open. The sound of happy-go-lucky, children's music blared from the kitchen into the foyer. There were toys strewn in the living room from one end to the other.

The half-eaten sandwich on the coffee table and the tilted-over tumbler lying on its side told April even more explicitly than her mother's words that, since Stephie's nanny had left to help her daughter, Gabe was having problems juggling being a CEO and a single parent.

Slipping off her jacket and tossing it over the arm of the sofa, April crossed the living room and stopped in the kitchen doorway. Three-year-old Stephie sat on her booster seat at the kitchen table, her hands, face and T-shirt covered with mustard as she finger-fed herself a piece of cheese from her sandwich. The smell of a burnt pot or pot handle filled the kitchen, and the top of the stove littered with pots looked worse than the interior of the living room. A stack of dishes toppled over in the sink and cereal boxes, toys and glasses with milk rings littered the counter surface!

In a quick glance she took it all in, then focused on

Gabe who was sitting at the other end of the table, a sandwich to his right, a laptop to his left, its power cord straying from the table to the receptacle on the counter.

He clasped his cell phone to one ear while he held his other ear shut. As he spoke into the phone, he had no idea she was standing in his kitchen.

In his black T-shirt and blue jeans with his muscular arms, tanned skin and incredibly broad shoulders, he looked more like a rugged outdoorsman than an entrepreneur. His strong facial features drew her gaze to them. Thick dark-brown hair fell over his brow, and she longed to brush it back, hug him, and be enveloped by his strong arms.

But she'd forfeited that right years ago when she'd fled her deepening feelings for him... when he'd become interested in her sister Vanessa and married her. And now—

With each passing day, April was more aware of the vow she'd made to her sister before she'd died eight months ago and the secret that could shatter Gabe's world.

When Gabe clicked off the phone and glanced toward his daughter, he spotted April standing in the doorway. A smile turned up his lips until his green gaze met hers. Then the smile slipped away.

As he stood, Stephie glanced over her shoulder and spotted April. With a whoop of glee, she slid from her seat onto the floor and ran across the room. "April! April! I missed you."

April caught her niece, gathering her into her arms. "I missed you, too, sweetie."

Since Vanessa's death, April had flown from Boston to Cedar Corners, Virginia, at least every other weekend to check on Gabe and Stephie. But for the past two months, her job as a financial analyst had taken her on a special assignment to Los Angeles.

Gabe switched off the iPod on its dock on the counter. "Your blouse will never be the same," he said with a grimace as he looked at the mustard on April's white-knit top.

His gaze as it swept over her, from her light-brown bangs and softly-waved hair, down her boat-necked top and her practically brand-new sneakers, sent color to her cheeks. Was she imagining it, or did there seem to be more than casual interest there tonight?

April tickled Stephie's tummy, and her niece giggled. "A hug from this little imp is worth it. The top will bleach." Meeting his gaze again, she said, "Mother called me." Although her mother had sold her house in Cedar Corners a few months ago, Winnifred kept in touch with Gabe regularly.

Gabe held out his arms to his daughter, and she went to him. As he carried her to the sink, he said, "When Winnifred called, Stephie was crying and I—" He stopped. "I was having a night similar to this one. Tonight I started a chicken dinner but the chicken burned—" He stopped again as if the explanation was self-evident.

"Mother said Evelyn went to her daughter's."

Gabe turned on the spigot. "She'll be gone the last two months of her daughter's pregnancy and then another six weeks. The problem is finding someone I trust who is as capable as she was. I haven't had any luck yet."

"You've been working from home the past few weeks?"

After he took a clean wash cloth from a drawer, he held it under the spigot and wrung it out with one hand. "It's been hectic, but we're managing." He glanced at her. "I thought you were in L.A."

"I was, but I finished the assignment there and took the vacation time I've never used. I have about six weeks, so if you need me to fill in until you can find a nanny, I'm available." She said it lightly as if it were no big deal, as if it didn't matter if he needed her help or if he wanted it.

Gabe was a proud man. She'd hurt him a long time ago, and she couldn't bear the thought of ever hurting him again. But to be honest with him, she might have to. She wished Vanessa had never confided her secret…or confessed her sin. Maybe April wanted to help Gabe out now and take care of Stephie so that she could make a decision that she had postponed making for the past eight months.

Gabe had gone still at her words. "I can't ask you to give up your vacation time for us, April."

"You don't have to ask. I'm offering."

The sound of slowly running water was the only sound in the kitchen until suddenly the cell phone lying on the table beeped.

Gabe gave it a dark look.

Reaching out to her niece again, April took Stephie from his arms and set her on the counter. "Go ahead and take it. I'll clean her up."

His gaze held April's for a few seconds, then he moved to the phone.

April could tell the conversation troubled Gabe from the few remarks he made. And the terminology he used told her it was business. When he hung up, she asked, "A problem?"

"More than one. And I should take care of it now. But…"

"I can clean up Stephie *and* put her to bed if it comes to that."

When he studied April with deep green eyes that seemed to see right through her, she felt she had to say more. "I want to help, Gabe. Really." He hadn't let her do much more than play with Stephie on the weekends she'd visited them.

Rubbing the back of his neck, he glanced at the laptop on the table. Then he eyed her again. "It would help if I could get back into the office and get caught up before a real catastrophe hits. But if I don't find someone to watch Stephie soon and you want to leave, just say the word. I don't want to tie you down."

If there was a deeper meaning to his words, she couldn't find any hint of it in his expression. When she'd left years ago to take an assignment overseas, she'd told him she couldn't date him any more because she couldn't be tied down. He hadn't asked her to stay. After all, they'd only dated for two months. He certainly couldn't have professed undying love. She wouldn't have believed him if he had.

She carefully wiped Stephie's hands. "You won't be tying me down. I have no commitments for the next six weeks." Then she smiled at him. "And my neighbor is watering my plants."

Seeing Stephie was as clean as she was going to get from the washcloth, Gabe crossed to the sink and lifted his daughter into his arms.

Pushing a stray blond curl behind her ear, he explained to her, "April's going to play with you for a little while and help you get ready for bed. You listen to her, okay?"

Stephie nodded, then asked, "Can she read stories?" With her sparkling hazel eyes and blond ringlets, she could have been a cherub in anyone's heaven.

"At least one," he assured her. Then he gave her a hug, and she gave him a loud smacking kiss.

The tableau Gabe and Stephie presented made April's chest tighten and her heart ache because she knew she had to make the most difficult decision of her life and possibly change Gabe's relationship with Stephie forever.

How could she ever tell Gabe that he wasn't Stephie's father?

****

After taking April's luggage to the guest room, Gabe strode down the hall to the den that served as his home office. He heard the sound of Stephie's chatter as his daughter and April played in the family room. He'd told her he'd deal with the state of the house later. His daughter always came first and April knew that.

Sitting at his desk, he woke up his desktop computer and heard April's voice as she answered one of his daughter's many questions.

April.

When she'd appeared in his kitchen with her sparkling brown eyes, soft skin and concerned expression, he'd had to remind himself about the vow he'd made years ago to keep distance between them. They'd only dated a short while after he'd hired her firm to help him develop a financial plan to make his burgeoning electronics business a company to be reckoned with. April had been assigned to his account, and from the moment he'd laid eyes on her, there'd been chemistry between them. As he'd gotten to know her better—her intelligence, her warm humor, her sweetness—he'd wanted to get a lot more serious than dates that ended with inflammatory kisses at the front door. She and Vanessa had both lived with Winnifred then, in a mansion on a hill overlooking the rest of Cedar Corners.

But one night, after their kiss threatened to lead much further, April had pulled away, told him she was accepting a job with a firm in Boston, and she would be leaving the States for a year to work in Singapore! She'd been determined to put half a world between them and chase career success. He'd decided if she could leave so easily, they might have chemistry between them, but her feelings obviously went no deeper.

He'd tried to forget her by working day and night. But one evening he'd bumped into Vanessa, and she'd entertained him with her vivacious personality that suited her work in advertising. She'd flirted with him, he'd felt flattered, and they'd started seeing each other. As they dated, he realized he wanted to settle down and start a family. He and Vanessa planned their wedding. When he saw April again a few weeks before the ceremony, he'd told himself he was over her, that he was committed to Vanessa and the future they could have. He and April would be polite in-laws.

But something had happened to his marriage—something that his commitment to it and a child couldn't fix. He was still trying to figure out what had gone wrong, why Vanessa had withdrawn from him until he'd felt only duty and responsibility and nothing more.

Now he turned his attention to his work, determined to concentrate on *it* rather than history he couldn't change.

It was almost ten p.m. when he'd finished in his office and climbed the stairs two hours later. No sound echoed downstairs or up. The hall light shown brightly on the hardwood floor, and more light spilled from his daughter's room.

The door was ajar, and when he pushed it opened, he stopped. April was curled on Stephie's bed, her arms around his daughter as they both slept. On one hand April held a plush blue dog puppet. Stephie had it cuddled under her chin. Gabe had never seen the puppet before and supposed April had brought it for his daughter.

Stephie's single bed was hardly big enough for the both of them. April was still dressed, and he supposed she'd fallen asleep unexpectedly. Crossing the room, he watched her for a few moments. Her long eyelashes fanned her cheeks. Her hair fell across her chin. His pulse beat more rapidly and he suddenly wanted to hold her in his arms.

The thought startled him and made him tap her on the shoulder and call her name.

Her eyes fluttered open and she started, then turned her head and saw him. Self-consciously she brushed her hair from near her lips and gently extricated herself from Stephie's hold, leaving the puppet by her niece's arm. Sliding her feet to the floor, she straightened her top. When she did, the soft knit pulled over her breasts, and Gabe's gut tightened.

As April stood, they were very close, close enough for Gabe to smell her perfume, close enough to know the pink glow on her cheeks was natural, close enough to realize he was still attracted to her in an elemental way even after all this time.

Quickly he reached for Stephie's covers and pulled them up. After a kiss on his daughter's forehead and a murmured goodnight, he switched on the night light.

After April preceded him out of the room, he motioned toward the guest room. "I put your suitcase in there." His gaze held hers and awareness built up between them once more.

She took a breath, then smiled. "I won't be able to

get to sleep after that little nap. I'll come downstairs with you and help you clean up."

April had stayed in his guest bedroom during her overnight visits since Winnifred had sold the family home. She'd spent most of her time with Stephie, and he'd treated her like a guest. If there had been undercurrents between them, they'd both ignored them. So why was tonight different? Why was his awareness of her so palpable?

Because she'd be staying more than one night. Maybe lots of nights.

Gruffly he responded, "You don't have to help me clean up. I don't expect that, April."

"Are you going to fight every attempt I make to help you while I'm here?" she asked simply.

"Is that what I'm doing?"

"Yes. And I wonder if it's because—"

"Because…" he prompted.

She hesitated only briefly. "Because you're too proud to accept help. Or maybe you just don't want to accept *my* help."

April's honesty was one of the qualities he admired and respected about her most. "I don't expect you to take Evelyn's place, and I don't expect you to be a housekeeper."

"How about if I'm just Stephie's aunt, and I pitch in wherever I can?"

She seemed determined not to let his pride—or anything else he was feeling—get in the way of assistance he obviously needed. Finally he gave in. "You win. I'll even let you vacuum, if that's what you want to do."

She laughed, and the sound of it brought light into a place in his heart that had been dark for too long.

He motioned to the stairs in a cavalier gesture. "Ladies first."

With a smile, she preceded him downstairs.

They worked in the family room first, gathering up toys and cleaning off sticky surfaces. As April picked up two coffee mugs, she said, "I think I'll wait until tomorrow to vacuum. Then you won't feel guilty about it."

He looked up at her, and when he saw she was teasing, he gave her a wry grin. "Don't you know a man's house is his castle and he wants to think he can run it with one hand tied behind his back?"

She shook her head. "Maybe we'll have to try that while I'm here. I'd love to see you cook with one hand tied behind your back."

This time *he* laughed. "I gave up on trying to be

Top Chef."

A few minutes later they went into the kitchen and started on it. As they cleared the table, April's stomach grumbled.

"Did you eat supper?" Gabe asked.

"Nope. Airlines don't serve meals anymore unless you fly in first class. I didn't."

"I don't have much in main courses, but there are cookies in the cupboard." He liked them as much as Stephie.

"I'll wait until we're finished here."

Gabe unplugged the laptop and took it to his office. On his return to the kitchen, he helped April clean off the counter. They both reached for the box of cereal at the same time, and somehow their hands got tangled. He found his fingers covering hers and lingering much too long. When he looked into her dark brown eyes, he saw emotion there. But it almost looked like...fear? Why would she possibly fear him?

Pulling her hand out from under his, she avoided his gaze and busied herself.

"April."

She faced him.

Suddenly the distance that had grown between them over the years seemed uncomfortable and unnecessary. "Maybe we can be friends again," he suggested. "We were once." They had been more than friends and on the verge of something tremendously important.

His heart beat at least three times until she responded, "I'd like that."

But she moved away from him, rinsed the dishes in the sink and quickly loaded the last pot into the dishwasher. Before they could even begin the process of becoming friends now, she said, "I think I'll skip the cookies and go on upstairs."

His kitchen was once more clean and organized, and there was no reason why she shouldn't. And no reason why he shouldn't let her. "I'll see you in the morning, then."

Nodding, she said softly, "Good night, Gabe."

As he watched her leave the kitchen, he realized becoming friends again wouldn't be as easy as saying the words…or as easy as it had been the first time.

After he turned off the light in the kitchen, he went to the foyer and heard no movement from upstairs. Feeling drawn to the hall closet, he pulled out the stack of photo albums, including his wedding album on the bottom. He hadn't looked at that one in years. An envelope under the wedding album fell to the floor. When he picked it up, he assumed it was filled with pictures he'd forgotten to insert in one of the albums.

Crossing to the living room, he laid the albums on the coffee table, sat on the sofa and began with the wedding photos. As he studied each picture, he remembered the day and the sense of satisfaction that he and his new wife were building a foundation for the future. April was in those pictures as Vanessa's maid of honor.

The two sisters *were* vastly different. Vanessa's beauty was model-perfect, her blond hair always professionally styled, her nails freshly manicured. However, not long after they'd married, he'd realized she was spoiled. She liked to be the center of attention and when she wasn't, she'd pout. April, on the other hand, possessed a quiet beauty, her light brown hair soft and natural around her face, a touch of lipstick her only make-up. She didn't crave attention and she didn't seek it.

He paged through a second and third album— Stephie's christening, her first birthday, play times in the park. And he noticed there were fewer and fewer pictures of him and Vanessa together.

Finally, picking up the envelope, he opened it and

found three snapshots. Apparently they'd been taken at a Christmas party. He recognized Vanessa's co-workers from the advertising firm where she'd worked in nearby Richmond. The first two snapshots were generic, employees milling around the punch bowl. The third…was a picture of Vanessa in a sequined red dress, dancing with Larry Powell.

Gabe checked the printed date on the back of the photo. They'd been married a year then. He'd been busy enlarging his company, opening a second store in Richmond, then a third in Leesburg. A problem had developed with renovations on the building there, and he'd missed the Christmas party.

Vanessa's and Larry's faces brought his gaze to the photos again. They were dancing…close…looking at each other… Once more Gabe examined the other two photos. Larry and Vanessa were in both of them.

They'd worked together, his common sense told him.

They'd died together, a new suspicious voice added.

That icy night, Larry had picked up Vanessa to take her to a meeting with their client. Gabe remembered the phone call, the hours at the hospital, the few times Vanessa had regained consciousness to speak to April and to beg him to always take care of

Stephie. But Vanessa hadn't survived, and neither had Larry Powell.

Inserting the pictures back into the envelope, he shoved them into the top photo album. On the surface, his marriage to Vanessa had seemed ideal—a successful couple doting on the child they both loved. But it had been much less than ideal.

The clock on the living room mantel struck midnight. Carrying the photo albums to the closet, he shoved them back on the shelf where they belonged.

****

When April awoke, the room was pitch-black. Though the digital clock by her bedside read four a.m., she was completely alert. Just what she needed—middle of the night insomnia. But even as she thought it, she knew the problem wasn't insomnia. It was her reaction to Gabe. When his fingers had covered hers tonight, she'd felt her body quiver. It was too painful to long for his touch, yet to know she couldn't have it. She'd left, and he'd fallen in love with and married her sister. Anyone could see why. Vanessa was the beautiful one, the vivacious one, the ambitious career woman, the wife and mother who'd handled all the roles perfectly. Gabe didn't know his wife had been unfaithful. He didn't know Stephie was Larry Powell's child.

Gabe's relationship with Stephie was so precious. How could she ever tell him the truth?

Pushing back the sheet, she slid out of bed and opened her bedroom door.

April headed for the bathroom to get a drink. But even with the small night light burning above the sink, she missed Stephie's step stool and tripped over it, making a clatter. The master suite had its own bathroom and Gabe had outfitted this one for Stephie.

April switched on the bathroom light and was rubbing her foot when she heard Gabe's bedroom door open. She thought about scurrying back to her bedroom for her robe, but it was too late for that.

When he appeared at the bathroom door, she murmured, "I'm sorry I woke you…" Her voice trailed off as her gaze settled on his bare chest. Curly brown hair sprung up the center whirling around his nipples and lower down to his navel—

"Need anything?" he asked, his eyes touring her shimmery pink nightgown.

She felt extremely self-conscious. When she'd

stayed overnight before, she'd never forgotten to put on her robe. And she'd never bumped into him in the middle of the night. As he gazed at her, she felt her nipples harden.

Flustered, she brushed her hair away from her cheek. "No. I just wanted a drink of water. But I should have turned on the light. I forgot about the stepstool."

"Trouble sleeping?"

She shrugged, wishing her mother had never sold their house in Cedar Corners to move to Florida, wishing Gabe would go back to his room instead of showing concern. "Maybe if I read a little, I'll be able to fall back to sleep."

He moved Stephie's stool to the place where it belonged next to the sink. "Would music help? You can use my iPod."

Grabbing onto anything that would get them out of the confined space of the bathroom, she said, "That would be great."

He motioned for her to follow him.

As April stepped into his bedroom, she realized again how briefly they were both dressed. His navy sleeping shorts didn't leave much to her imagination.

The king-sized bed with its rumpled sheets took

up half of the room. The double cherry-wood dresser and chest, along with two-bedroom chairs and an oval cherry table forming a sitting area, took up the rest. She followed him to the chest of drawers.

Opening the top drawer, he took out the iPod—this one different from the one on the dock downstairs. "I don't know if there's anything here you might like." He switched it on and tapped on the music menu.

When she stepped up beside him, she could almost feel the heat of his skin. She'd heard his shower running before she'd fallen asleep. Now she could smell soap and male, and as she glanced over at him, the matt of hair and the expanse of his chest made her long to touch it.

Focusing her attention on the music playlists, she said, "These are great! I forgot you like Coldplay as well as Blake Shelton and…" Her voice trailed off as she glanced up at him. His gaze caught hers and held it, and she felt her breaths become shallow and faster.

She could feel the electricity between them as surely as if tiny sparks were stinging her. Could it be her imagination? Could she really see desire in his eyes?

Gabe took a step away. His voice was gruff as he

said, "I like a little bit of everything. Except jazz."

April's hand trembled as she gathered the ear buds along with the iPod. Then she crossed to the door and paused. "I'm going downstairs to make myself a cup of tea. Sometimes that helps me unwind. I'm sorry I've kept you up."

As she started down the hall, Gabe called, "April?"

She stopped and turned.

"You might want to wear a robe downstairs. Some of the windows don't have shades."

Her color heightened as she murmured, "I'll keep that in mind." Instead of continuing down the hall, she ducked into her bedroom.

Closing his own door, Gabe swore.

He hadn't meant to embarrass her. But if she was going to stay, she couldn't go roaming around like that...

He closed his eyes for a moment seeing her creamy arms, the few freckles along her neckline, her soft fluffy hair caressing her nape. He grew hard with desire.

Opening his eyes, warring with needs that he thought had long died, he swore again.

Chapter Two

Dressed for work in a white shirt and striped tie, Gabe entered the kitchen early Friday morning before Stephie was up, the smell of coffee and bacon welcoming him. "You didn't have to make me breakfast," he said as he crossed to the carefully set table. April was supposed to be on vacation!

"I have to eat, too, don't I?" she asked with a smile.

"And you cook yourself a breakfast like this every morning?"

Her cheeks flushed. "No, but this wasn't a chore, Gabe. I like to cook when I have the time."

They needed to set some ground rules or he'd feel as if he was taking advantage of her kindness. His gaze passed over her snug, worn jeans that fit her slender figure as well as the red-and-white striped, long-sleeved knit shirt that molded to her breasts.

He remembered kissing her years ago, touching her last night and her response to both—she'd pulled away. His gaze settled on her lips, perfectly pink without lipstick. "You're on vacation and you could be having fun somewhere."

"How do you know I won't have fun here?" An impish twinkle danced in her eyes and it was hard for him not to respond to it...or to the sweet garden scent of her standing so close.

"April, whether you have fun or not isn't the issue. What if I pay you?"

She brought a plate with strips of bacon and scrambled eggs to the table and set it at his place. "Don't be ridiculous."

"I don't want to owe you."

The silence between them seemed to stretch interminably until finally she said, "You won't owe me if you look at my staying here as a gift."

The kitchen was alive with more than her offer. There was a pulsing awareness that wouldn't quit. The tenderness in her expression, the curve of her cheek, the inviting softness of her skin drew his hand to her face. His thumb traced the line of her chin.

"It's a special gift, April, and I'll accept it under one condition."

"What?" she murmured.

"That you take time for yourself. That you spend evenings however you want. I know you still have friends in Cedar Corners. I don't want you to feel tied to us." He dropped his hand before he slipped it under her hair to finger it.

"It's a deal," she replied softly.

Why did he suddenly want to hold her more than he wanted to breathe? Calling on the self discipline he'd honed for years, he gestured to her plate still on the counter. "Good. Now we'd better eat before all this good food you prepared gets cold."

When she moved away from him, he was sorry. But he could be even sorrier if he acted on an impulse for old times' sake.

As he sat at the table, he tried to push his awareness of her aside. "I've enrolled Stephie in preschool. I thought it would be good for her to interact with other children her age."

An only child himself, his mother had died when he was ten. It had been he and his dad until Carl Chronister had suffered a fatal heart attack when Gabe was in college. He'd intended to become stable financially, then find a woman to love who wanted a large family as much as he did. But after Stephie was born, Vanessa hadn't been interested in having more children. In fact, for the last year of their marriage, they'd slept apart more than together.

"Do I need to take her to school today?" April asked. "I don't have a car seat in my rental."

"She goes on Tuesday and Thursday mornings. But if you need to drive anywhere, take Vanessa's car. It has a car seat. I always use the SUV, and I've thought about selling her sedan. But I just haven't gotten around to it. We can turn in your rental tomorrow."

April was quiet for a moment. "All right. It does seem silly to keep the rental while I'm here."

Motioning to the kitchen window, he added, "Remote is on the sill. Insurance card is in the glove compartment."

As Gabe dug into his eggs, keeping his eyes off of April, the lull in their conversation grew uncomfortably long. To fill the gap, he asked, "Do you think Winnifred's happy in Florida?"

"I don't know. Every time we talk, she tells me about all her activities. She wouldn't admit it, but she was lonely in that big house here after Vanessa and I moved out."

"She was fortunate it sold so quickly." There was something he'd wondered about for years. "What was your father like? I know he and Winnifred divorced when you and Vanessa were teenagers, but whenever I asked her about him, she just said she never knew him very well…that after the divorce, he didn't try to stay in touch."

April took a few moments before answering, and Gabe wondered why. But then she said, "That about sums it up. His work took him away a lot, and we hardly ever saw him."

"He was an expert at international law, wasn't he?"

April nodded. "Whenever he came home from a trip, he'd bring a stack of postcards to show us the places he'd been. I guess he thought that would make up for him not telling us about them."

She didn't sound bitter, just disappointed. He sensed there was a lot she wasn't saying.

As he reached for another strip of bacon, so did April. This morning their fingers didn't touch, but their gazes held for a few seconds.

Then April looked away, set the bacon on her plate and picked up her glass of orange juice.

They might both want to be friends again, but

something was standing in their way. Maybe if April stayed long enough, he'd find out what it was.

****

April could still feel the trail of heat from Gabe's thumb on her face after he left for his office. She had to get a grip on her emotions. Every time he got that close she wanted more. She'd run from him years ago because of intangible fears. She'd come here determined to face those fears as well as her feelings for Gabe. Yet it was so complicated now. Could Gabe ever forgive her for leaving five years ago? Could he forgive her for keeping Vanessa's secret?

If she held back the truth, Gabe and Stephie's relationship would be safe.

Built on a lie? her conscience asked.

She didn't have the answer. She'd loved her sister. Before she died, Vanessa had explained how she'd been racked with guilt since she'd discovered she was pregnant, how she'd cut off her affair with Larry before Stephie was born...but that they hadn't been able to stay away from each other. However, before she died, her main concern had been Stephie, and Gabe's feelings for their baby. That's why April had promised she wouldn't tell Gabe the truth…not ever.

But now whenever she looked into Gabe's eyes, she felt compelled to tell him the truth. Then she thought of her niece and held back. At the hospital the night of the accident, April had learned Larry Powell had no living relatives. If Gabe's feelings towards Stephie changed, the little girl would have no one else to give her the unconditional love a child deserved.

April had to be sure she was making the right decision no matter what the cost was to herself.

Once her niece awakened, the morning passed quickly. But after Stephie finished her milk at lunch and put down her cup she asked, "Go see Daddy?"

"Daddy's working."

"But I wanna see him."

Though she had never read child psychology books, April would bet that if a child's world was disrupted, she'd want to hold onto something or someone stable. April was sure Stephie missed her mother's presence, and now Evelyn's.

"I don't think your dad would mind a visit from us. Why don't we stop at the bakery and take him something for a snack? You can pick out a dessert for supper."

"Cupcakes!" Stephie decided with a wide smile.

April laughed. "Cupcakes, it is."

Cedar Corners, once a farming community, had grown into a mid-sized town with new residential developments cropping up periodically, school districts expanding, and more businesses moving in. Yet it still retained its small town flavor with lots of community events like its summer strawberry festival, periodic spaghetti suppers served at the fire hall and its Fall Festival taking place this weekend. Tomorrow, crafters and artists would line the downtown streets which would be barricaded against traffic.

April drove through the town and turned into the parking lot of an office building. Gabe's complex of offices was located on the third floor. With three stores open now throughout Virginia, he'd needed a central headquarters from which he could oversee and coordinate. After she parked, she locked Vanessa's car, and took her niece's hand as they crossed to the glass door and rode in the elevator to the third floor.

Everything from the plush sand-colored carpeting to the cream and chocolate leather chairs in the small reception area shouted quality and success. April had never seen Gabe's offices before.

Going to the middle-aged woman seated behind a

huge desk, April kept Stephie's small hand in hers. "We're here to see Gabe Chronister."

"Do you have an appointment?" the woman asked as she peered over her reading glasses.

With a pleasant smile, April returned, "Does his daughter **need** an appointment?"

The receptionist glanced down at Stephie. "Uh, no, I suppose not. Let me buzz him." Picking up the phone, she announced to Gabe that he had visitors. A few moments later, he came down the hall to the desk and saw them.

April's heart raced. He was even more handsome and powerful-looking in a suit than jeans. The cut of his navy jacket seemed to emphasize his broad shoulders.

Scooping Stephie up into his arms, he said, "I didn't expect to see you quite yet."

"She missed you," April explained, wondering if she'd done the right thing by bringing Stephie here.

But Gabe didn't seem disturbed about it. "Let's go to my office. Mrs. Canton, hold all my calls."

Gabe's office was a masculine domain. Book shelves filled with manuals and binders lined one wall. His L-shaped desk faced a sitting area with a leather couch and chair. A painting of a rustic farmhouse and a scene of horses grazing hung on the wall.

He took Stephie to the couch and sat her on his knee. "So you missed me?"

Stephie bobbed her head and clutched a waxy white bag in her hand.

"I suppose you miss Evelyn, too?"

Again Stephie nodded.

"Did you have fun with April this morning?"

His daughter looked at April and grinned. "We colored. An' we played outside."

"What did you bring?" Gabe tapped Stephie's bag but his gaze slid over April in her turquoise blouse and slacks.

"Cookies. I tol' April you like chocolate chip."

He laughed, a deep rumble that vibrated through April. "And maybe you want to split one?"

Stephie grinned. Then she asked, "Are you comin' home soon?"

"Pumpkin, I have to work until supper. But after supper you and I can play ball till dark. Okay?"

Stephie hopped off his lap and opened the bag of cookies. "Okay."

Rising to his feet, he took April's elbow and guided her across the room to the picture window. "Is everything all right?"

"I think so. She's used to you…and Evelyn. But I'll keep her busy. I wasn't sure if I should bring her here."

Gabe leaned closer to her. "Don't hesitate to call me or bring her by."

His hand was still on her arm, his head so close to hers that she could smell his cologne.

There was a quick rap on the door and then it opened. A man with close-cropped gray hair and tortoise-shell glasses barged in. "Gabe, the latest set of numbers is good. Damn good. We should—" Seeing April and Gabe's hand on her arm, he blushed. "Oh, I'm sorry. I didn't mean to interrupt."

Gabe took a step away. "It's okay, Jim. You're not interrupting. April is Vanessa's sister. She's taking care of my daughter until I find a new sitter."

Finally catching a glimpse of Stephie quietly eating a cookie on the sofa, Gabe's associate looked relieved. "This can wait. Give me a buzz when you're free."

April watched the man leave the office, Gabe's words still ringing in her ears. *April is Vanessa's sister.*

Was that *all* she was to him? Could she be more? Could she compete with Vanessa's memory?

"April?"

Gabe must have asked her a question. "I'm sorry.

What did you say?"

"Is something wrong?"

How could she tell him she still had feelings for him? Vanessa had only been gone for eight months… "No. Nothing's wrong. I was just thinking I should get back so I can start supper."

His gaze was probing until Stephie came running to him with his half of a very large cookie. He took it from her with a wry smile that almost broke April's heart. As he wiped a few crumbs from Stephie's mouth so gently, she prayed she'd make the right decision for all of them.

****

Gabe threw the big red ball to Stephie and she scrambled after it. He wondered what April was doing. She'd been very quiet during dinner, talking to Stephie more than him.

When the kitchen door opened, he did a double take. April was wearing a jogging suit. Bright blue. It fit her like…a second skin. Every curve was defined. And they were all very tempting.

Forget it, Chronister.

Why wouldn't his body listen to his good sense?

As she approached him, he noted the sweatband holding her hair.

She smiled at Stephie, then said to him, "I'm going for a jog. It usually takes me about an hour."

He couldn't keep his gaze away from the fit of her top over her breasts, her leggings hugging her hips. "It will be dark soon. Be careful you don't slip on the leaves." The whole yard was covered with them, and he'd have to rake soon.

"I'll be fine. I'm used to leaves. We have them in Boston," she teased, then took off under the trellis, along the flagstone path that led to the front yard.

He watched until she was out of sight.

After he put Stephie to bed, Gabe took a shower. Back in his bedroom, he reached for his sweat suit, looked out his bedroom window and forgot about getting dressed. Having finished her run, April was stretching on the front lawn. Fascinated, he marveled at the flexibility of her body, the beautiful long contours of her arms and legs. When a sleek black sports car purred down the street and pulled into his driveway, he saw her slowly come to her feet and pull the headband from her hair.

Nicholas Chandler was one of Gabe's best friends. He and Nicholas had hung around together in high school, and they still did. April had met and spoken with Nicholas over the years. Now as Nicholas strode up the walk, the post light threw beams on his black hair. He'd tugged his tie down and turned back his white shirt cuffs. The smile that spread across his friend's face made Gabe wish April was wearing something other than that jogging suit! Nicholas had a reputation with women and was dubbed in Cedar Corners' scuttlebutt as its most eligible wealthy "hunk."

Gabe dressed quickly and went downstairs. Sitting together on the sofa, April and Nicholas were talking as if they were old friends.

As if they want to be new friends?

April's hair was loose and waved around her face as it sometimes did when the weather was damp. Her cheeks were rosy. From the night chill, her run, or from talking to Nicholas? She was turned toward his friend, one leg curled up on the sofa and Nicholas' arm rested along the back, his hand very near her shoulder.

When Gabe moved into the room and crossed to them, their conversation stopped and he felt as if he'd interrupted.

"April's been telling me how much she enjoyed

Singapore," Nicholas said with a smile.

Gabe wondered if his friend had been charming April or simply listening to her. "You were there last year, weren't you?" Gabe asked casually.

"That's what I was telling her. We were comparing notes."

They'd have a lot of notes to compare if Nicholas was interested in April. In a flash Gabe realized he didn't *want* Nicholas to be interested in April. Or April interested in him.

"April is taking a vacation and filling in for Evelyn," Gabe explained.

His friend glanced at April again. "I've advised her to do her exercises in the backyard for the rest of her stay. The intriguing sight of her stretching could stop an ambulance…or every man who drives by."

April blushed and Gabe's gut clenched. Maybe Nicholas was teasing, but maybe he was trying to score points. From the look on April's face, he'd succeeded.

"Thank you," she murmured and avoided Gabe's gaze.

"You're welcome," Nicholas replied with a twinkle in his blue eyes.

April straightened on the sofa. "Nicholas just got

back from Chicago."

"Another buyout," Nicholas explained.

"Hostile?" Gabe asked, all too aware of successful business strategies.

"Nope. This one was friendly," Nicholas said with a sly smile.

April looked from one man to the other, then stood. "I'll let you two visit."

But Nicholas stood, too. "I can't stay. I'm on my way to an appointment with my real estate agent. I've decided to put a contract on a house."

The fact that Nicholas had stopped by to deliver the news in person meant he was excited about it. If he was going to buy a house, maybe he was finally going to settle down. "Where is it?" Gabe asked.

"Out Country Mill Road."

"The old Falworth estate?"

"That's it. Never thought I'd give up the convenience of the condo, but...I don't know. I want more permanence than that."

"Are you ready for permanence?" Gabe wondered what had brought Nicholas to this decision.

His friend shrugged. "I guess I discovered I need roots...though I never thought I'd want them." He checked his watch. "I've got to get going. April, it was good to see you again. If you stick around, stop in at Constellation Enterprises. You've never seen my offices. I'll show you around the financial department and you can give me your opinion on the numbers of a few of my more speculative ventures." Clapping Gabe on the shoulder, he asked, "Are we still on for basketball next Saturday?"

Gabe glanced at April. "I think I'll pass this month."

"Don't change your plans because of me," April said.

"I told you, I won't take advantage of you. You should do what you want on weekends."

"I'm here, Gabe. I don't mind."

When Nicholas' brows arched at their interchange, Gabe told him, "I'll let you know."

Nicholas crossed to the foyer. "You know where to reach me." After a final wave, he closed the door behind him.

The silence lasted until Nicholas backed his car out of the driveway.

"I'm going to get a shower," April said.

She would have passed him but Gabe caught her arm. "Are you going to visit Nicholas at Constellation?" He didn't know why he was asking.

Maybe because he'd rather she'd visit **his** offices again rather than Nicholas Chandler's.

"I might."

Gold lights danced in her brown eyes and he wondered if his friend had put them there. "Be careful, April. Nicholas can make the phone book sound like the best-seller you're dying to read."

Her brows arched. "I don't know what you mean."

"Nicholas has money and looks and knows how to use both."

"He's your friend!"

"It's because he's my friend that I know he's lethal with women."

"You think I can't tell practiced charm from sincerity?" Her voice was indignant.

"I don't know. What was Nicholas using on you?"

She blinked, and then asked, "Why do you care *what* he was using?"

The pulse of tension between them threatened Gabe's self control, as did the scent of April, the spirit in her eyes, and the sweet curve of her lips. Without thinking of consequences or the past or the future, he pulled her into his arms, and his lips came down on hers.

All hell broke loose…or was it all heaven?

A fire rose in Gabe so high, so hot, so huge, that it burned his reservations and resolve to red sparks that reignited and added to the inferno. Yet the height of his desire was dizzying, almost euphoric. The touch of April's lips was as inflaming as her taste was sweet. Lips on lips wasn't enough. His tongue laved her lower lip until she opened her mouth, until she wrapped her arms around his neck, until her soft breasts pressed against his chest. His hands explored her back and as she reached up to him, her top bared her midriff. Her skin was like hot satin and he could almost imagine burying himself inside her.

He wanted satisfaction. He wanted completion. He wanted release.

Trembling began deep within April like a ripple of excitement so powerful it didn't know where to vibrate first. The touch of Gabe's lips on hers started a chain reaction of sensation that joyously danced through her, teaching her, thrilling her, arousing her. He was giving her the gift of a desire so strong that she forgot about time and place and secrets. Her world was filled with Gabe and the pleasure he could give her…the pleasure he wanted from her.

But as Gabe's kiss led her deeper into passion, as his tongue swept her mouth with hungry demand and his hands caressed her with the intent to explore more, she knew she had to stop him. She knew she had to stop herself. Because she wasn't being true to him. Honesty was everything between a man and a woman. They didn't have that. She couldn't give him honesty without destroying his life.

Unlocking her hands from behind his neck, she dropped them to his shoulders and pushed away.

He looked stunned, and she suddenly wondered if he knew who he was kissing or if he'd returned to a place where he'd been with Vanessa. "I'm not Vanessa, Gabe."

His green eyes pierced her. "You don't think I know that?"

"Do you? Or are you just missing her and a wife's touch?"

"So you think I kissed you because you're convenient?"

"Am I?"

He stared at her, then raked his hand through his hair. "Maybe you are. Maybe I slipped back in time and forgot you have a career to return to. Or maybe I just wanted to prepare you for what Nicholas might dish out."

"I'm not that inexperienced!" she flared, suddenly

angry at him, herself and, most of all, Vanessa. Knowing she didn't want Gabe questioning her about her love life because she'd have to admit he was the only man she'd ever kissed, she said again, "I've got to get a shower," and turned away from his searching regard.

But he clasped her arm once more. "Be careful, April."

His fingers scorched her, and she wasn't sure if he meant for her to be careful around Nicholas…or around *him*.

Pulling away, she climbed the stairs and felt Gabe's gaze on her back. She wanted to cry. She was torn between falling in love with Gabe all over again, or hurting him and Stephie…maybe irreparably.

She had to find the courage to make the choice.

Chapter Three

The overcast sky and sweeping gray clouds didn't dim Stephie's mood as she sat in her car seat in the back of Gabe's SUV, chattering to the puppet April had given her.

Glancing over her shoulder at her niece, April smiled. The three-year-old was a bundle of sunshine even on a cloud-filled day as they drove back to Cedar Corners from returning April's rental car in Richmond. The half-hour drive seemed much longer because of the silence between her and Gabe. They'd exchanged polite surface conversation throughout the morning.

Gabe cast a quick look at April. "Would you like to stop downtown at the craft fair and get some lunch? The rain's not supposed to start until early evening."

"Sounds good to me. One year they had a petting zoo. Stephie would like that."

"Almost as much as the cotton candy. We'll have to make sure she doesn't see that until after we get her something more wholesome to eat."

"Like hot dogs or pizza?" April teased.

Gabe smiled. "Don't forget the hamburgers, candy apples and chicken corn soup."

"Not to mention apple fritters."

They both laughed this time, and the sound of it seemed to relieve some of the tension. But only some of it. Last night's kiss still hung between them, its effects lingering even under their laughter. April wondered if it had shaken Gabe as much as it had shaken her.

As Gabe drove into the downtown area of Cedar Corners, men women and children were strolling along the streets to and from their cars. A red hybrid pulled out of its parking place along the side street, and Gabe took the spot. After he unlatched Stephie from her car seat, he locked the SUV, and they each took one of Stephie's hands. She bounded along between them, hopping up and down, the hood of her red windbreaker flopping along behind her. As the cloudy day breeze picked up, April was glad she'd worn her jacket. Gabe had opted for a forest green cable-knit sweater instead of a jacket and looked as rugged and handsome as always.

The craft stands and vendors along the street, most of them under canopies, offered a variety of items, from hand-crocheted doilies to leather goods. Residents of Cedar Corners and visitors, could take the food they bought inside the community center to the long tables to sit and eat it. Gabe spoke to several people he knew as they went inside with their food, and April felt the strong sense of community Cedar Corners had always fostered. She'd missed it living in Boston. The community center was noisy and there wasn't much opportunity for conversation. April was just as glad, because every time her eyes met Gabe's, they both seemed to pause, aware of each other in a way they hadn't been the past few years.

After they all finished lunch, Stephie raised her arms to Gabe, and he lifted her and carried her as they walked along the stands stopping every now and then.

The petting zoo was set up in the park a block from the town square. Stephie giggled as she ran her hand through the wool of a lamb and petted a lop-eared bunny. When she stood beside a large sheep dog who was as tall as she was and whispered something in his ear, Gabe leaned close to April. "I might have to think about getting her a dog. Maybe next summer."

"What kind?" April asked, curious as to whether Gabe had put much thought into it.

"I've heard Labs are good with kids. But I want Stephie to help take responsibility for the animal so I have to make sure she's ready."

"Are *you* ready?" April joked.

With a wry shake of his head, he said, "I'll admit, it probably sounds better in theory than in practicality. But she loves animals."

After Stephie had her fill of petting the animals, Gabe took her hand and led her toward a circle of canopies situated around the park's gazebo. At the first stand, Stephie could see into the glass case where antique jewelry lay inside. She pressed her nose up against the glass. April looked down through the top, and a gold locket caught her eye. It was beautiful—round, almost as big as a silver dollar with delicate etching around the edge.

The woman at the stand saw April's interest. Reaching inside the case, she brought the locket out for April to examine.

April held it in her palm. It was heavy. "It's beautiful," she told the vendor as she opened it and saw the place for pictures inside. "How old is it?"

"1920's," the woman answered.

April handed it back to her. "It really is beautiful. But impractical for me." She wore business suits most of the time and little if any jewelry. A lapel pin now and then. If she bought the locket, as beautiful as it was, it would probably lay in her jewelry chest more than she would wear it. It was meant to be worn with loved ones' pictures inside. Maybe someday…

When she looked over at Gabe, she saw that he was watching her. She gave a little shrug and a smile, and they moved on.

"April. April Remmington. Is that you?"

April turned in the direction of the woman who was calling her and saw a high school classmate of hers sitting at a booth selling ceramic items on the other side of the pathway that wended through the park.

Seeing that Stephie had a firm hold on Gabe's hand, April crossed over to Barb Mahoney and gave her a big smile. "How are you? It's been years since I've seen you."

Barb nodded vigorously. "Our last high school

reunion. How have you been?"

The breeze suddenly became more vehement and tossed April's hair. "Busy," she answered.

"I heard about Vanessa and I'm sorry. One of the kids was sick and I couldn't get to the viewing or the funeral."

"Thank you," April said softly. "It's been a difficult time but we're managing."

Obviously not wanting to linger on the subject, Barb said, "I heard you are doing a lot of traveling."

Gabe came up beside April with Stephie in his arms, nodded to Barb and picked up a small ceramic dog that Stephie pointed to.

Answering Barb's question, April nodded. "It's part of the job. At least for this firm, and I do enjoy it."

Buttoning her trench coat against the wind, Barb smiled wistfully. "I heard you spent a year in Singapore. What a wonderful opportunity. Do you know what I'd give to travel like that instead of doing dishes and laundry and cleaning up after three kids?"

April could see Gabe was listening. Singapore was a subject they didn't bring up because it marked the end of the relationship they might have had.

"It was a terrific experience," she said honestly. She

felt more than saw Gabe frown.

"Are you planning on going anywhere else exotic any time soon?" Barb asked.

Careful about her answer, April shook her head. "It's not in my immediate plans."

"Well, if I had the chance, I'd take it," Barb said. "You're not married. You don't have any kids or anything tying you down. You should enjoy life as much as you can before you do."

It was all in a person's perspective, April supposed. In high school all Barb had talked about was getting married and raising a family. Now looking back, maybe she wished she had done things differently. It was ironic that April regretted leaving. Her gaze met Gabe's and she could see he was processing what he'd heard. He thought she'd left because she was running toward her career. But she couldn't tell him yet that she regretted leaving, not until she figured it all out. She still wasn't sure exactly what fears had driven her away.

Before she could even say goodbye to Barb, a fine mist started to fall.

"We'd better get back to the car," Gabe said, his voice even.

April didn't know anyone who was as good at

hiding what they were feeling as Gabe. Would he care if she took a position in London that her boss had mentioned. Would he miss her? He hadn't asked her to stay before and she doubted if he would now.

As they hurried to the crossing light at the square, the heavens opened and the mist became a downpour. April looked down at Stephie and saw her little face crinkled up against the rain. Automatically April unbuttoned her jacket and swung it off, holding it over her niece.

"April, you are going to get wet," Gabe started.

"Better me than her."

Sweeping Stephie up into his arms, jacket and all, he jogged across the street with April at his side. They didn't stop until they reached the SUV. As quickly as he could, he unlocked the doors and settled Stephie in the back seat. April climbed in the front, dripping wet.

Gabe was pretty wet himself as he climbed in and looked over at her.

She'd worn a pale blue oxford blouse with her jeans with the top two buttons of the button-down collar opened. Now the cotton clung to her, molding to her arms, shoulders and breasts. Shivering, she pushed her wet hair behind her ear.

Gabe reached into the back seat for her jacket and handed it to her. "Put this back on. Maybe it will keep you from getting chilled until we get home."

The jacket warmed her a little and as she looked over at him she smiled. "What we need are some towels." Gabe's sweater was soggy, and a droplet of water from his brown hair rolled down the side of his cheek. She longed to reach across and swipe it away…

But in a quick motion, he started the car and turned on the heater. "Unfortunately, I don't keep any in the car. Let's see if we can beat the traffic out of here before we get caught in a real traffic jam."

Lots of fair goers were running to their cars anxious to escape the rain. Fortunately, Gabe pulled out and drove down the street before too many cars did the same. Soon he was on the outskirts of the downtown area heading toward the development where he lived. With the heat blowing from the car's heater, he glanced over at April, remembering how she'd given his daughter her jacket. Sometimes she was so selfless with Stephie. More so than Vanessa. Vanessa would have considered her own comfort first.

Where had *that* thought come from? Vanessa had cherished their daughter as much as he had. Yet she was so very different from April. Vanessa wouldn't have given that locket a second look. Gabe could tell April had liked the piece of jewelry. She certainly had the funds to buy it. But April always thought about whether she needed something or not, and apparently she hadn't needed another piece of jewelry even though the locket had lit up her eyes and brought a smile to her face. That's why he'd picked up the vendor's card. He needed to show April somehow that he appreciated her help. That locket might be exactly the thing he was looking for.

After he pulled into his driveway and quickly pressed the garage door opener, he drove into the garage. But before he could even open his door and flip off the heater, April had slipped from the car and was already helping Stephie out of her car seat. He opened the door to the kitchen and waited for April to pass through, Stephie cuddled in her arms.

"I want to get her dry," April said as if she needed to explain.

"I'll light a fire. We can all use some warming up."

Gabe had shrugged out of his damp sweater and touched a match to kindling when Stephie came bounding into the family room. April was right behind her. She was still wearing her wet clothes, although she'd changed Stephie into a dry pair of overalls.

"All warm again?" he asked his daughter.

Seemingly unfazed by the rain, Stephie nodded and ran to the miniature table and chairs in a corner of the family room where there was a can of crayons and a stack of coloring books. Closing the mesh curtain on the fireplace, Gabe crossed to April.

"You've got to get out of those clothes." He could see her bra through her blouse emphasizing soft curves that he suddenly wanted to touch very much. She needed to get out of those clothes for *his* well-being as much as hers.

"I'm on my way. I washed my sweat suit this morning and it's in the laundry room in the dryer."

"I could have gotten it for you," he mumbled.

"I'll be fine, Gabe. A little bit of rain isn't going to hurt me."

"A lot of rain," he said with a grimace, noticing the mole on the left side of her cheek usually hidden by her hair. Her bangs were drying, but the rest of it was still wet even though it looked as if she might have tried to towel the moisture out of it. He was too intensely aware of everything about her. He smelled perfume mixed with rain and his gut tightened.

"How about some hot chocolate after I get

changed?" April asked. "You can sit in front of the fire. Maybe help Stephie build something with her blocks."

"That's your idea of a relaxing Saturday afternoon?" he asked with a raised brow.

"That's exactly my idea of a relaxing Saturday afternoon."

As he gazed down at her, he could remember her taste, the feel of her in his arms, the softness of her hair. He remembered everything about last night's kiss in vivid detail, so vividly in fact, his body was aching to hold hers close again. Her deep brown eyes sparkled with the knowledge of kissing him too, and the idea of doing it again was so very tempting. He almost bent his head. He almost pulled her close.

Once upon a time Gabe had dreamed of a Saturday afternoon just like this, sitting in front of a fire with his wife and a child. But April wasn't his wife. She was April. And although she loved Stephie, this was a novelty for her and he suspected too many days of it and she'd get bored.

"Go get changed," he said again gruffly. "Stephie and I will have the hot chocolate ready by the time you're dressed."

As April turned to head for the laundry room,

Gabe realized he had to learn to enjoy the moment...because sometimes moments were all a person could ever have.

****

After April pulled the clean laundry from the dryer and dumped it into the wash basket on Monday afternoon, she banged the door. Ever since Gabe had kissed her on Friday night, he'd kept his distance, almost acting as if he didn't want to talk to her or be around her. She was used to the distance. It had been there since she'd left for Singapore. She'd hoped if she stayed here now...

Gabe had been a faithful, committed husband who loved his wife dearly. He was still grieving and he might never, ever get over Vanessa. She had to face that fact. Maybe after their kiss, he'd felt guilty as if he'd betrayed his wife. *That* was ironic. A little devil in her head whispered, *If you tell him about Vanessa's betrayal, he might turn to you.*

But April shook the thought away. She didn't want Gabe on the rebound. She didn't want to be a substitute. She wanted him to love her for herself, but that might not happen. If she told him the truth, he might blame her for hiding it. There were no easy solutions here. Every decision could lead to an emotional mine field.

What she needed was some perspective, and getting out of the house might provide that. She loved being with Stephie and Gabe but the complications of their future relationship was sometimes overwhelming. To make good decisions she had to be clear-headed and that meant not thinking about Stephie and Gabe twenty-four hours a day.

Stephie was taking a nap when April checked the clock in the kitchen, wondering if Nicholas might be in his office. She took out her cell. He said he would give her a tour of Constellation and she'd like that. If he was serious about wanting her opinion on a couple of ventures, she knew analyzing the numbers would help focus her attention for a while.

After his secretary asked who was calling, she put April on hold. A few moments later, Nicholas' voice came through loud and clear. "Hi, April. What's up?"

She'd always felt comfortable with Nicholas, and she didn't need to heed Gabe's warning about his friend. She knew Nicholas' charm was part and parcel of what he did for a living. After all, his business was negotiation.

"You said you'd give me a tour of Constellation. I thought I'd take you up on it."

He paused for a moment but then said, "Well, good. When do you want to come over? I spend a lot of time here."

She laughed. "I need to watch Stephie till Gabe gets home, so it would be after that or else a couple of hours tomorrow morning after I take her to preschool."

"Tonight's good for me. I have meetings tomorrow morning."

"Are you sure you don't mind staying late?"

"Late? I'm not sure exactly what that is. Many nights I'm here till midnight. Just come on over after Gabe gets home. I don't need to know exactly what time. I'll be here."

After April thanked Nicholas and said goodbye, she speed-dialed Gabe.

"Anything wrong?" Gabe asked.

His voice was as deep as Nicholas' but it had a resonance for her that always made her breath catch. "Nothing's wrong. I made an appointment with Nicholas to tour Constellation this evening and I wanted to make sure it was okay with you."

In the silence she could hear the beat of her heart

until Gabe asked, "And if it isn't?"

"I can make it another night."

"I see. Tonight should be fine," he said in a clipped tone. "I can make sure I'm home by five. Don't worry about supper for Stephie and me. I'll take her out somewhere."

"I can put a casserole in the oven—"

"Go take your tour, April. We managed before you came and we'll manage after you leave. It's fine."

After April hung up the phone, she felt a definite disquiet, but she pushed the feeling away. Gabe had told her her evenings were her own, and she didn't need his paternal attitude about any association she might have with Nicholas.

Returning to the laundry room, she began folding the clean clothes. She picked up one of Gabe's T-shirts. She smoothed her hand over it, then made quick work of it, ignoring the intimacy she felt at folding a man's underwear.

****

Gabe was unzipping Stephie's jacket when April came into the kitchen and crossed to the window sill to pick up the remote to the car. He'd left with

Stephie earlier, thinking April would be gone when he returned. But apparently she'd taken great care dressing. He hadn't seen her in anything but jeans since she'd arrived. But tonight she wore a pants suit—narrow-leg black slacks and a royal blue boxy jacket trimmed in black.

"I thought you'd be gone," Gabe said gruffly.

"I'm working on it," she replied as she picked up the remote.

Stephie held out her cup to April. "Want some milk shake?"

They'd gone to Stephie's favorite fast food restaurant. A vanilla shake was always part of the order.

"No thanks, sweetie. You drink it. Was your hamburger good?"

Stephie nodded, and Gabe thought April knew Stephie's habits as well as he did. "Are you having dinner with Nicholas?" he couldn't keep himself from asking.

"No. I grabbed some yogurt." Her gaze met Gabe's. "This isn't a date. He's just going to show me around his offices."

"You look as if you're dressed for a date."

"A girl gets tired of jeans, Gabe. And business

suits. Besides, I didn't think jeans would be appropriate. This is sort of middle of the road."

It wasn't the middle of *any* road. It made her look pretty and sexy and everything he didn't want her looking with Nicholas.

As Stephie plopped her milk shake on the table, she knocked off a few e-mails that Gabe had stacked there. One was a reminder for Stephie's preschool open house. "I know I told you your evenings were your own, but Thursday night Stephie's teacher is having an open house. I thought you might like to go along."

Lifting her coat from the back of one of the kitchen chairs, she also picked up her purse that was lying on the corner of the table. "Sure. I'd like to go along. But for now I'd better get going. I don't want to hold Nicholas up if he doesn't want to stay late tonight."

As April passed him, Gabe wanted to catch her arm. He wanted to tell her not to go. He wanted to warn her again to be careful with Nicholas.

April gave Stephie a hug and told her she'd see her in the morning, and Gabe could only think of one thing to say. "The roads are still wet. Drive carefully."

It had been raining most of the day, and leaves

covered many of the roads. It was an appropriate comment to make.

But April looked at him as if she were searching for something. Finally she said, "I'm always careful. I probably won't be gone long. I'll see you later."

Then she went down the short hall past the laundry room to the garage. Gabe heard the garage door open. He heard the car start and April back out. When the garage door came down again, he wished he had said something else, something more important, something that she'd remember when she was with Nicholas. But that was foolish.

Holding out his hand to his daughter, he said, "Let's go get you ready for bed. Then we can watch that new movie we bought. Okay?"

She smiled up at him, and he decided she was all the sunshine he'd ever need in his world.

After Gabe put Stephie to bed, he worked in his office for a while. He checked his watch—nine p.m. It was funny—the house felt empty with April not in it. There had been so much strain and distance between him and Vanessa that they were rarely in the house together. But the past few days with April…

He'd gotten used to seeing her playing with Stephie on the floor in the family room or making something in the kitchen. Getting used to her being here was *not* a good idea.

When he went to the living room and switched on the TV, his mind wasn't on the images on the screen. As 9:15 came and went, he thought about calling Constellation to see if April was still there.

As he was about to reach for the phone, he heard the garage door going up. His lack of interest in the TV program changed to avid regard, and he was totally engrossed by the time he heard April's steps outside the family room.

When she came in, he hardly gave her a glance, but he commented, "Long tour."

She didn't sit but stood at the end of the sofa. "It was more than a tour."

Her words brought his gaze to hers. He switched off the TV as he looked for signs that she'd had more than a casual evening with Nicholas. "You went somewhere with Nicholas?"

After studying Gabe for a moment, she shook her head. "No. He showed me the office complex and the day-care center that he set up last year. He'd done lots of research on the benefits of having a day-care center on site for its employees. I took a look at some of it, then when he found out that I hadn't actually eaten dinner, he ordered in some Chinese."

"And after dinner?" Gabe prompted.

The golden light he'd seen in her eyes after their last kiss flared again. "What do you want, Gabe? A play-by-play?"

"I want to know if Nicholas made any moves on you."

"Nicholas was a perfect gentleman. We looked over the numbers for a few businesses he wants to buy."

Gabe stood, feeling as if he wanted to pace the room but controlling the urge. "And that took all this time?"

"I'm over twenty-one, single and free to come and go as I please. I don't appreciate being grilled even if you are well-intentioned because you see Nicholas as some kind of threat to me. He's not. In fact, we have a lot in common. He has two tickets for the symphony in Richmond on Saturday evening, and asked me if I'd like to go. I told him I would."

Gabe's heart beat faster as he tried to deny how much he disliked the idea of April and Nicholas going on a date. And that's what it would be. But as she'd said, she was a free agent. There was nothing he could do about it. She probably went to the theater and symphony all the time while she was in Boston. "If Nicholas shows you a good time, I guess you won't be bored while you're here."

"I'm never bored while I'm here, Gabe." She moved away from him toward the doorway. "I'm going to go upstairs and read for a while. I'll see you in the morning."

She was gone before Gabe could tell her goodnight.

Chapter Four

The children played in Mrs. Norman's preschool as the parents milled about the learning center. April was studying the selection of games the children could choose from, but her mind was on the silent drive over here with Gabe. Ever since she'd told him she was going to the symphony with Nicholas, he'd been too polite and, most of the time, remote. Not with Stephie, of course. He gave her warmth and smiles and plenty of attention.

Now Stephie was showing Gabe a wooden puzzle with large pieces. As always he paid complete attention to her, listening carefully to what she had to say. Would he still be as loving and free if he knew Stephie wasn't his daughter? Just how much would the truth change his relationship with her?

April had never had much of a relationship with her own father, and she missed his presence in her life. When other kids talked about the things they did with their dads on weekends, April had always felt different. Her father had traveled so much of the time, and when he was home on weekends...

He'd gone out—without their mother. Oh, her mother and father had attended charity functions together, dinners for civic causes, parties among a circle of social elite. But most of the time her father went out alone. Only he wasn't alone. But it wasn't until she was in her teens that she realized *that*.

A friend of hers had told her she'd seen her father in a restaurant in Richmond over the weekend—with a woman. Wanting to give Stanton Remmington the benefit of the doubt, April had assumed it was a business dinner. But then she'd answered the phone late one night, and a woman had asked for her father. When she'd told the caller her father wasn't there, the woman wouldn't give her name or the reason for calling and April had started putting two and two together—whispers behind her mother's back at the Tennis Club, rumors that circulated throughout the high school and got back to her. Her father didn't have business dinners with women on Saturday night. No, he took them to fine restaurants and to the theater. As the years went by, his affairs became more blatant, but her mother never said a word. She'd never talk to April about it, and April hadn't said anything to her.

Not knowing how she'd tumbled into that train of thought, she was roused out of it by two children who ran by her chasing each other. There were parents and children everywhere so she didn't know who they belonged to. As she glanced around, she saw Stephie sitting on the floor with a classmate putting puzzles together. Gabe was talking to Mrs. Norman who'd given a brief presentation when they'd first arrived.

April couldn't keep her gaze from Gabe. He looked casually handsome tonight in a tan sweater with an off-white oxford shirt underneath. His slacks were camel-colored. She'd dressed in a pale-blue sweater and matching light-wool slacks. When he'd first seen her after she'd changed, she'd thought she'd seen male admiration in his eyes. But she couldn't be sure of anything where Gabe was concerned right now.

Suddenly a woman joined his conversation with Mrs. Norman. She was pretty, blond and wore a red sweater-dress that hung a few inches above her knees. April's intuition went on alert as she watched the woman whose gaze trained on Gabe's face more than Mrs. Norman's. She also moved a little closer to him.

Wanting to get a better look at the woman's expression, April moved toward the table with the punch bowl and cookies and dipped herself a cup of punch. The two children who had run by her before ran by again. But April was more concerned with the smile Gabe was giving the woman and his apparent interest in her, especially when Mrs. Norman moved away to talk with another parent. The woman in the red dress kept speaking to Gabe as if they were old friends. Maybe they were. Maybe they were more than friends. After all, it wasn't as if Gabe told her about the details of his life or confided in her his innermost thoughts.

She wished he would.

Deciding to find out who the woman was instead of guessing, April took a step forward just as the two children who had been chasing each other made a complete circle around the room, ran into her, then the table holding the punch and cookies. It was like a comedy of errors. Not only did April spill the cup in her hand as she tried to catch the little boy who had rammed into her, but on its way to the floor, the punch bowl splashed red punch all over her light-blue slacks. The room had gone silent at the crash. The two children froze, and all eyes were on April.

She could make a fuss, but the damage was already done. From the look on the two little boys' faces, she expected that they knew they'd be facing consequences in a few minutes. Touching them both gently on the shoulder so they'd know she wasn't going to scream at them, she said, "Go the bathroom and get me a bunch of paper towels. Fast. But don't run."

After a few blinks at her, they took off at more than a walk but less than a run. She shook her head.

A moment later, Gabe was at her side. "Are you all right?"

She couldn't help but roll her eyes and smile. "More all right than those kids are going to be when their parents' are through with them, I bet."

Gabe had taken out a clean white handkerchief. Pulling a folding chair from the side of the room, he dragged it over. "Take your shoes off."

She'd worn black leather flat shoes with a strap over the instep. The hem of her slacks, her hose and her shoes were all splattered with the red punch, and she could feel already, it was getting sticky.

Mrs. Norman came running over with towels. "I don't know how much these are going to help, but at least they'll sop it up. I'm so sorry this happened. I couldn't get to those two in time."

"There's nothing to be sorry about. It was an accident. But if we don't mop up the floor, you're going to have lots of sticky feet trampling across the room for the next week."

There was amusement in her tone, and Mrs. Norman stopped trying to wipe up the mess and looked at April. "Thank you for taking this so calmly. Your clothes are probably ruined."

April had learned long ago that some things are more important than clothes. The children who had run into her were doing their best to mop up some of the spill, too. Farther away from April, their parents were standing over them with stern expressions.

She said, "I didn't want to call any more attention to them in front of everybody. After all, it was an accident. When adults have accidents, we take it as a matter of course. But children... They're just doing what they do naturally."

Returning with her shoes, Gabe handed them to her. Then he knelt down and swiped at her foot with a wet cloth. "This isn't going to fix the problem," he said, "but it might help you be a little more comfortable driving home."

Gabe's ministrations were adept, quick and gentle. She could smell his cologne, and when his fingers brushed over the arch of her foot once, twice and then around her ankle, she could feel the heat from his touch all the way to her face.

As he started on her other foot, Stephie came over and sidled up beside her. "You're a mess."

April laughed. From the mouth of babes. After she gave Stephie a quick hug, she tapped Gabe on the shoulder. When his gaze met hers, she wanted to…to what? Tell him the truth about his daughter? Tell him she was falling in love with him all over again? Tell him she was as afraid now as she had been five years ago?

Instead, she took a deep breath and held out her hand. "I can do that, Gabe."

He studied her silently, then handed her the towel and held his hand out to Stephie. "C'mon, Pumpkin. Let's see if we can find a janitor's closet and something that'll help get this cleaned up."

April almost breathed a sigh of relief as he moved away.

A short time later after April had tried to clean her slacks in the bathroom and Mrs. Norman had apologized again, they drove back to Gabe's. April kissed and hugged Stephie good-night, then showered. When April finished in the bathroom, Stephie's night light was on, so she knew Gabe had gone downstairs. With her stained clothes over her arm, she headed downstairs, too, and straight to the laundry room. But Gabe was in the kitchen, sitting at the table with a glass of milk and a package of chocolate cookies.

"I guess you didn't get any punch and cookies at the open house," April said with some amusement.

He grinned. "Nope. By the way, I forgot to tell you. While you were in the bathroom cleaning up, the parents' of the twins said you should buy yourself a new outfit, and they'll be glad to pay for it."

"They don't have to do that."

"They felt responsible."

"I know, but I'm going to see if I can get the stains out, then send them to the cleaners."

Gabe tilted his head, and she could see that he was wondering why a woman who could buy as many new clothes as she wanted, would worry about removing a stain. "This is one of my favorite outfits, Gabe.

Mother gave it to me two Christmases ago. So if I can save it, I want to do that." Then she took her clothes to the laundry room.

After she cleaned them up the best she could and went back to the kitchen, Gabe motioned to the second glass of milk he'd poured and the bag of chocolate sandwich cookies. "Join me?"

With a smile she sat beside him. "You know I can't resist these any more than you can."

He dipped one into his milk. "Yes, but *you* like to take them apart. I don't."

He was right about that. Twisting a cookie apart, she stole a quick glance at him. "Mrs. Norman's school looks as if it has a lot to offer." Not knowing how to lead into her question any other way, she asked bluntly, "Who was the woman talking to you just before the punch bowl fiasco?"

Plucking a cookie from the pack, he gave her a curious look. "That was Debra Evans. Her daughter was putting puzzles together with Stephie. She's a single mother. And very considerate. After Vanessa died, she brought me a casserole about once a week."

Considerate or moving in on a handsome, eligible man? But April couldn't voice those thoughts. "She's very pretty."

After dipping another cookie in milk, Gabe ate it. "Yes, she is."

April wanted to tell him to be careful, to realize that the woman probably wanted more than just to feed him. But then she remembered his warning about Nicholas and how *she'd* reacted. April realized she was jealous of this woman she didn't even know. Instead of just being protective, had Gabe been jealous of Nicholas, too? If so, did that mean he had feelings for her?

It was a ray of hope and gave her something to hold on to. She dipped half of the cookie she had divided, then popped it into her mouth. Maybe after she went to the symphony with Nicholas Saturday night, she'd find out if Gabe was jealous. And if he was...

Then maybe they *did* have something to build on.

****

Guarding Nicholas zealously, Gabe matched his opponent's movements step-by-step and feint-by-feint. Nicholas wasn't getting away with anything today, not if Gabe could help it. Their friendly game of basketball had become something more than a competition for points. As Nicholas moved to the side, Gabe blocked him. As his friend pivoted and dribbled, Gabe was right there.

Finally, trying to stare Gabe down, Nicholas asked, "What's gotten into you today?"

"We play for points, and we play to win. Don't we?" Gabe asked as his gaze didn't leave Nicholas for a second.

"A beer isn't worth the effort you're putting into this today," Nicholas answered.

Low man out always bought the winner beer at the local watering hole, where after the game Gabe and Nicholas caught up on what had happened since their last game or else just watched their favorite teams battle it out on the big-screen TV.

Gabe kept remembering the fact that Nicholas and April were going out tonight. "Want me to ease up?" He backed off a little, but still watched Nicholas carefully.

"Not on your life," his friend goaded with a smile as he tried to push past him.

But Gabe was ready for him, and when Nicholas tried to make a long shot, Gabe caught the ball in one hand, dribbled fast to the basket and scooped it in easily.

Nicholas shook his head. "I'll buy the beers. There's no getting through or around you today."

Knowing he should feel a great deal of satisfaction, yet not experiencing any exhilaration, Gabe tossed the ball to Nicholas. "Giving up already?"

"When have you ever known me to give up?"

Too true, Gabe thought. "Strategic retreat?" he suggested.

Nicholas walked over to the bench and picked up his towel and slung it around his neck. "Not exactly. But I thought after a beer, you might want to see my new house. I'm having some work done before I move in, but I have the key."

"So you're really going through with it?"

"Closed on it yesterday," Nicholas said as he sat and pulled on his sweat pants. "The house has been empty for so long they were glad to wrap up the deal quickly. Let's get those beers," he suggested. "Then you can tell me how good it will feel to be a land owner."

Gabe wondered if Nicholas was really ready to settle down. And if he was, who would he settle with?

****

Listening for the doorbell, April attached gold hoop earrings to her ears. Her black dress could easily be made casual or dressy. Tonight she was dressing it up by slipping into black pumps. She'd thought about canceling tonight. She knew Gabe would be relieved. But *why* would he be relieved? She wanted him to put it into words. But she knew he wouldn't. And even if he did…

Would she reveal what she knew about Stephie?

She'd thought by staying here, her decision would become clearer. But instead, it seemed to be getting more complicated. Maybe going out with Nicholas tonight would help her put everything into a better perspective. She couldn't be impulsive. She couldn't do anything until she was sure of her course. Because once Gabe knew the truth, all of their lives could be changed forever.

When the doorbell rang, April tossed her coat over her arm and picked up her purse. But she was only half way down the stairs when Gabe reached the door ahead of her and let Nicholas inside. Gabe had returned home about an hour before and told her Nicholas had showed him through his new house. But that was about all he'd said. Now his expression was neutral.

Nicholas was dressed in a charcoal suit with a white shirt and black and gray tie. He was a handsome man. Yet as her gaze went to Gabe in his T-shirt and jeans, she wished she was going out with him tonight.

As she reached the bottom step, Nicholas said, "You look terrific."

"So do you," she returned with a smile. It was easy talking to Nicholas. Easy joking with him. He was like the big brother she always wished she'd had.

"Where are you taking her?" Gabe asked.

"A new Italian restaurant. Do you like Italian, April?"

"Sounds good to me," she said as she came to stand beside him. "I'm ready whenever you are."

Nicholas took her coat from her and held it so she could slip into it.

Gabe just glowered.

As she tucked her purse under her arm and belted her coat, she said to him. "I have my key. So don't feel you have to wait up."

"But you *are* planning on coming home tonight?"

She felt heat rise quickly to her cheeks, whether from embarrassment or frustration with him, she wasn't sure. "I plan to be home around midnight, but if my plans change, I'll let you know."

Nicholas cleared his throat. "I'll take good care of her, Gabe. You don't have to worry."

"That's what I'm afraid of," Gabe mumbled.

Opening the door, Nicholas let April precede him outside. Then he closed it behind them.

Once they were in the low-slung car with its leather scents surrounding them, Nicholas looked at her. "I think you and I need to have a talk. But I'd rather do it over a glass of wine than while I'm trying to concentrate on the road. How about some music? Mozart or easy listening?"

"Easy listening," she answered, suspecting exactly what Nicholas wanted to talk about.

At the restaurant with its fine linens, lit tapers secluded in hurricane lamps and quiet atmosphere, Nicholas waited until they ordered before he folded his arms on the table. "Okay, now tell me what's going on with you and Gabe."

She wasn't about to evade Nicholas' question. Gabe was his best friend. But she wasn't sure how to answer, either. "I wish I knew," she murmured.

His brows arched. "He treated me like the enemy on the basketball court today. We both have a keen sense of competition, but there's been a change in his attitude lately, and I'm pretty sure it has to do with you. Did you agree to come tonight because you knew it would make Gabe jealous?"

"No! And I'm not sure jealousy has anything to do with it. He's acting like a father letting his teenager go out on a date for the first time."

Nicholas chuckled. "That's jealousy you're seeing, April. Trust me."

"He just feels protective. He—"

"What's going on, April?" he asked again.

She shook her head, and tears pricked in her eyes. Sometimes the secret she carried weighed her down so much she wasn't sure she'd ever be free of it. But when she thought of the consequences of revealing it, she accepted the weight of the burden. She'd like to confide in Nicholas, but she couldn't. At least not about that.

"I still have feelings for Gabe," she said honestly. "I regret leaving five years ago."

Nicholas studied her for what seemed like a long time. "Does he know?"

"No. I buried them and ignored them after I left until I believed Gabe was a part of my past. I treated him like a brother-in-law, and that's all he was. But lately, especially since I came back to take care of

Stephie, there's this…tension between us."

"You're afraid he's still in love with Vanessa," Nicholas suggested perceptively.

"Yes." She could say so much more, but she knew something about Vanessa that might change Gabe's feelings for his wife. But she didn't dare. Nicholas was too quick. Even the subtlest of hints could set his mind in the right direction. She didn't want that.

"This is touchy, isn't it?" he asked as if he understood.

"It's complicated."

"And you didn't come out with me tonight to make Gabe jealous. You just needed a little bit of breathing space."

"Something like that, but maybe…maybe I thought a little jealousy wouldn't hurt."

"You're an honest woman, April Remmington. That's rare these days."

"Not so rare if you know the right women."

He grinned. "Touché." After a pause, he said, "I don't have any advice for you even if you'd want it. I'm not sure making Gabe jealous is the answer. Time might be the only thing that helps here. But I can be your friend if you need one. It's been a very long time since I had a friend who was a woman."

She was sure there was a story behind that statement, and maybe if she and Nicholas really became friends, he'd tell her about it.

The waitress brought their orders and set them down at their places.

Nicholas picked up his fork and said, "Okay, no more serious thoughts tonight. Just some good conversation, good music and good food. Is it a deal?"

"It's a deal."

****

Throwing off the covers, Gabe sat up on the edge of the bed. He should have known sleep would be a lost cause. He'd watched TV until ten and read the newspaper until eleven. When April had told him she had her key, she was sending him a message. *Don't wait up*. Well, it was his house and his life and he'd damned well wait up if he wanted to!

The clock at the side of his bed said midnight, and he convinced himself he wasn't waiting up for April. He was just going to get a midnight snack. After he pulled on a pair of sweatpants that were straggled across his bedroom chair, he didn't bother with a shirt. Out of habit he peeked in on his daughter. She was sleeping soundly, curled on her side, April's puppet clasped in her arms.

The ceramic tile in the kitchen was cool under his bare feet, but he hardly noticed. Going to the refrigerator, he pulled out a dish of roast beef that had been left over from the night before. April was an even better cook than Evelyn had been. Vanessa hadn't liked to cook, and on weekends, they'd usually eaten out or ordered something in. Gabe thought again about the vast differences between the two sisters. It had been easy to see that Vanessa had grown up in wealth from the way she dressed to her expectations of the life style they should have. Gabe had worked hard to make that life style a reality. Vanessa's salary had gone mostly for her clothes and jewelry, vacations and extras that she felt they'd like. Once he'd gotten the three stores off the ground, providing everything she'd wanted wasn't a problem. No, money hadn't caused the deterioration of his marriage, but he still didn't know what *had*.

He'd taken a few bites of his sandwich and washed them down with hot chocolate when he heard Nicholas' car pull into the driveway. Instead of going to a window like he wanted to do, he made himself stay put and took a few more sips from the mug.

A few minutes later, April's key turned in the lock, and Gabe wondered if Nicholas had kissed her. She must have seen the light in the kitchen from the foyer, and she came in, unbuttoning her coat. Her cheeks were pink and her hair tousled, but that could be from the cool autumn air…or from a quick but passionate kiss.

"I didn't think you'd still be up," she said as she ran her fingers through her hair to straighten it.

"Supper was a long time ago." That was enough of an explanation for his midnight foray into the kitchen. "How was your dinner?"

"Very nice." Sliding out of her coat, she hung it over her arm.

"And the symphony?"

"That was nice, too. I'm going to hang up my coat—"

"But Gabe couldn't wait until she did. "And how was Nicholas?" Gabe rose to his feet and crossed the room to her. He wanted to see into her eyes. He wanted to see if anything important had happened tonight.

"Nicholas was…fine."

Her hesitation worried him. "How fine?"

Her eyes flashed as she said, "I told you before, I

don't like to be—"

"Grilled," he finished for her. "Yeah, I know. But I'm doing it anyway. Did he kiss you?"

Her gaze widened, her mouth parted slightly, and he didn't care if Nicholas had kissed her because he was going to kiss her now. She'd forget about Nicholas' kiss, if it had happened.

With only the thought of wiping another man out of her mind, his hand slid under her hair, and he brought her head to his. He thought he heard a small gasp right before his lips covered hers.

Not intending to keep the kiss chaste by any means, his tongue parted her lips. She was hot and soft and perfect, and he felt her tremble as his tongue stroked against hers, coaxing and seducing until she moaned and tightened her arms around him. Her dress against his chest pushed him into further awareness of their bodies joined together. His sweatpants weren't much of a barrier as he pressed into her, aroused and hungry.

Warning himself he was heading into very deep water, he broke the kiss and looked down into her eyes. "Did Nicholas kiss you?" His voice was husky and strained with the desire stringing his body.

Pushing away from him, there was no denying she

was flushed from their kiss and not anything else. But she also looked angry and maybe even hurt.

"No, he didn't kiss me, Gabe. Nicholas was a perfect gentleman."

The implication was clear. *He* had not just acted like a perfect gentleman. "I'm not going to apologize for what just happened, April. It's been building up since you came back."

"Did you slip back into time again?" she challenged, her shoulders straight, her chin up.

"No. But maybe I've decided that Nicholas' life style looks attractive, and now that I'm single, I should take advantage of it." If he started caring about April again, if he thought about her in terms of a future, she could fly out of his life the same way she had before. He wasn't ready to take that risk, not after everything that had happened.

But now April *did* look hurt, as if she couldn't stand to be in the kitchen with him. She picked up her coat from the floor from where it had fallen and avoided his gaze until she crossed to the doorway and turned and faced him again. "You try out whatever you'd like, Gabe, but just don't think you're going to use *me* as an experiment again."

When he heard her high heels on the steps, he

drew in a deep breath, then let it out. Picking up his glass and dish on the table, he dumped the remainder of his sandwich into the garbage and rinsed out the glass, leaving it in the sink. Not sure exactly what had gotten into him, in turmoil from emotions and chaos inside of him, he didn't even realize where he was headed until he got there.

At the hall closet, he again pulled down the photograph albums and took them into the living room. He searched for the envelope that he had shoved into one of them. When he found it, he paused for a moment, before taking the pictures out of the envelope. Then he slid them out and examined them, one by one, trying as hard as he could to use an objective eye, trying as hard as he could to find answers.

Larry Powell and Vanessa.

In the group pictures, the two of them were standing close together, smiling at each other…and talking. Other people were around, but you could draw a circle around the two of them and point out the fact that they looked as if they were a couple. Why was that? Was it their intense regard for each other? The soft smile on Vanessa's lips that Gabe knew well from their early days together?

His heart pounded faster as he studied the picture of Vanessa and Powell dancing. Larry Powell's hold on Gabe's wife looked a little too chummy for a colleague.

This Christmas party was a year before Stephie was born. He suddenly felt as if a lightning bolt had struck him. What if Vanessa had had an affair? How long had it lasted? Could he be sure Stephie was his?

He sat there for an interminable amount of time, trying to absorb the questions, let alone find the answers. Finally, he put the pictures in the envelope and put the envelope back in the photo album. Then he carried them to the closet and slid them onto the top shelf.

When he went upstairs, he opened the door to Stephie's bedroom and stepped inside. She was an angel, and he'd always thought she was *his* angel. What if they weren't related by blood? What if he wasn't her biological father?

Though the question was shocking and sobering, he did have an answer. Biology didn't matter. Stephie was his…forever. He was her dad, and he wouldn't let an unsubstantiated suspicion torment him.

Chapter Five

Pushing Stephie on the swing on Sunday afternoon, April watched Gabe as he raked leaves into pile after pile. They were pretending as if last night had never happened, yet they both knew it had. She'd made breakfast, then he'd taken Stephie for a walk. She'd gone for a run and when she returned, he'd made a plate of sandwiches. She'd mixed a chocolate cake to have with supper, and he'd gone outside to rake leaves. Oh, yes, they were avoiding each other, too.

The autumn day was cool, not cold, the sky a brilliant blue, and the sun yellow with pre-winter warmth. After she'd taken the cake out of the oven and set it on a rack to cool, she'd put on her jacket and went outside where Stephie was trying to help

Gabe rake with a miniature rake all of her own.

But when she saw April, she came running to her, and asked, "Push me on swing?"

As April pushed, Stephie stuck her feet out in front of her and giggled. The laughter echoed in the crisp air, and April knew Gabe heard it because he looked up from the end of the yard. She was too far away to see into his green eyes, but she remembered how they'd looked last night right before he'd kissed her— deep and dark and mysterious like the passion she wanted to know with him. The thought made her fix her attention on Stephie again and give her another push.

When April's niece tired of swinging, she slid down the sliding board a few times. Then April caught her by the hand and said, "Let's go see if we can help your dad put those leaves in the garbage bags."

With an "okay" Stephie ran toward Gabe, her blond hair glowing golden in the sunlight. April followed Stephie, walking instead of running. She didn't ask Gabe if he wanted help, but rather picked up one of the large black bags and began stuffing leaves into it. Soon Stephie joined her. But suddenly Gabe's daughter decided that throwing the leaves up in the air and watching them float down was a lot more inventive than packing them away.

"I think you're having a lot more fun than we are," April said after Stephie had done it a few times.

Joining in, she picked up a fistful of leaves, threw them up in the air and let them float down on her and Stephie.

Stephie laughed and so did she.

Both of them taking handfuls again, they threw them up and laughed as the leaves tickled their cheeks and landed on their jackets.

After Gabe propped his rake against the tall sycamore trunk, he crossed to them and teased, "I thought you two were helping."

"Helping," Stephie agreed as she took handfuls and threw them up, but not quite far enough to land on him.

"It looks to me as if you're putting them back where I found them."

Gabe needed a little fun in his life, and there was no reason why April couldn't teach him how to have it. Catching him off-guard, she swiped up fistfuls and threw them above his head. A few landed in his hair, the others on his shoulders.

He brushed them off and gave her a mock scowl.

"Two can play this game."

He not only filled his hands, but his arms with leaves, tossing the mound high in the air until they fell on all three of them. Stephie giggled and jumped into the pile, making them fly everywhere, while April retaliated by swishing a few towards him like a wave of water. He batted a few back and lifted an armful directly above her head and dropped them so they fell around her like autumn confetti.

She laughed again. "You're going to have to rake them up all over again."

"*We're* going to have to rake them up all over again."

Their gazes met, and his eyes danced with amused patience. It felt so good to be joking with him…and laughing. "I might help if you promise me we won't have to do this again next week when the rest of the leaves fall to the ground."

His grin was crooked and almost boyish. "We'll just let that batch blow away."

They stared at each other for a few moments, and she wondered what he was thinking. She thought about asking him, but then remembered last night. Gabe had told her what he was thinking then, and she hadn't liked it.

Deciding not to tempt fate a second time, she said, "I'll get another rake," and headed for the storage shed.

Gabe called to her. "April…"

She turned, not knowing what to expect. His expression was so serious for a few seconds, and then it changed as he said, "You have leaves in your hair."

She had a feeling that bit of news wasn't the reason he'd called to her. But if he wanted to keep the afternoon light, she could do that. "If you go look in the mirror, I think you'll find a few in yours, too."

She didn't wait to see if he ran his fingers through his hair but went to get the second rake, liking the feeling of working with him…liking being part of his life.

****

Rain splattered the windows late Monday morning. It had begun with the dawn and looked as if it would last all day. April had made Stephie breakfast, and they'd colored for a while, then read a few stories. But her niece's attention span seemed shorter than usual today.

Going to the kitchen door, Stephie said, "I wanna

go outside and play in the leaves."

They usually went outside in the late morning before lunch. But today even a short walk was out of the question. They'd be soaked before they went three feet. "We can't, sweetie. It's raining."

"I wanna go outside," Stephie said again, ignoring April's reason.

April crouched down to Stephie's eye level. "I'll tell you what. I think it's going to rain all day today, but tomorrow, if the sun comes out, we'll play outside a really long time. How's that?"

"I wanna go outside and play with the leaves," Stephie said stubbornly, and her bottom lip quivered.

Not spending long periods of time with Stephie, April had never been faced with her stubbornness before. "We're not going outside today," she said calmly, hoping her firmness would register.

It evidently did because Stephie's face fell, her chin quivered, and she broke into tears.

April was at a loss to know what to do so she did what felt natural. She put her arms around the little girl. "Sweetie, we *will* go outside again. I promise. Just not today."

But Stephie shook her head. "Daddy'd let me go out." Her tears continued falling and didn't stop, not when April stood, not when she tried to bring a smile to her niece's face with the new puppet, and not when she offered Stephie lunch. The sobs turned to hiccups and she was inconsolable.

Although April didn't want to bother Gabe at work, she needed some guidance. So she called him. When she explained what had happened, he told her he'd be home in fifteen minutes, and he was.

When he came in the door his daughter ran to him, her pout still in place. "Daddy, Daddy! I wanna go outside."

Scooping her up into his arms, he sat on one of the kitchen chairs and settled her on his lap. "It's raining outside, Pumpkin."

"But I wanna play with the leaves." Her lower lip trembled again and tears welled up in her eyes. Her expression would have melted April.

But Gabe seemed unaffected, and his tone was firm as he asked, "What did April tell you?"

Stephie cast a sideways glance at her aunt. "She said I couldn't."

"That's right. The leaves are messy and soggy and dirty from the rain. And it's damp and chilly. She doesn't want you to get all wet or get a cold."

"I *won't* get a cold," his daughter protested

defiantly.

Gabe didn't get caught up in arguing with her. He just returned to his previous point. "When I'm not here, you *must* listen to April. She knows what's good for you just as I do. I expect you to do what she says this afternoon, or you're not going to watch TV after supper tonight." He stood and placed her on the chair. "You sit there and think about it. I have to talk to April for a few minutes."

When he cupped April's elbow in his palm and guided her into the foyer, she felt the excitement of having him touch her, of having him close.

Keeping his voice low so Stephie wouldn't hear, he said, "She's testing you."

"She's never done that before."

"You've never taken care of her day after day before. She's just trying to find out how much she can get away with, and how often she can get her own way."

"She's usually such a little angel."

He gave her a wry grin. "*Most* of the time. But she can be stubborn and downright contrary with the best of them. Don't let those tears fool you. She can turn them on and off."

April shook her head. "So how can you tell when

she's really upset?"

"For one thing, she doesn't pout when she's really upset. And the tears don't stop and start like a faucet then, either."

"Being a parent is more complicated than I ever imagined. You do an excellent job, Gabe." There was honest admiration in her voice.

"Thank you for saying that, because sometimes I'm not so sure of how I'm doing. Parenting is a learning experience, and I often wish I had a manual. Unfortunately, kids don't come with instructions. Whether you know it or not, you'd make a good parent, too, April. Is that something you ever think about?"

Yes, she'd thought about it, especially since she'd been here with Gabe. She'd thought about parenting Stephie with him and suddenly realized how she longed to have his children.

But she simply said, "Maybe someday. For now I'll practice with Stephie. Do you have time to stay and eat lunch with us?"

He carefully canvassed her face, as if searching for more than what she'd said. But then he checked his watch. "I have a meeting at one, but I have time for a quick lunch."

As they returned to the kitchen, April knew she'd like to steal lunches with Gabe a lot more often.

She'd like to steal more than lunches. She'd like to steal his heart.

****

The next few days seemed to speed by as April took care of Stephie, and Gabe was later than usual one evening. There was a spirit of cooperation between them and no mention of Nicholas. Still, she'd caught Gabe looking at her several times when he thought she wasn't aware of it. She still couldn't be in the same room with him without her pulse racing.

He surprised her Thursday morning when he said, "I'll take Stephie to preschool today. After I drop her off, I think you and I should talk. Will you take a walk around the reservoir with me?"

"Sure," came out of her mouth before she could stop it.

Autumn was in its high glory as they drove to the reservoir. Although many leaves had fallen, many still clung to the trees in golds, russets and reds. With the approach of Halloween the following week, November cold would soon replace the cool, crisp air.

They drove in silence to the outskirts of Cedar Corners and the reservoir with its path surrounding it. Gabe parked and they climbed out of the SUV, still in silence.

She had to break it. "Do you come out here often?"

"Mostly in summer in the evenings, if I have a sitter. Walking out here helps me work off…everything."

By "everything" April guessed he meant the overwhelming grief after Vanessa died. Was that grief still holding him in its grip? Maybe Nicholas was right and all they needed was time. Did Gabe really want to emulate Nicholas' lifestyle? That would be hard with a daughter.

As Gabe walked beside April along the path, the sun was warm on her shoulders. The only sound was the call of birds.

Gabe suddenly said, "You seem to enjoy watching Stephie. Do you?"

"I love taking care of her. I see the world differently when I'm with her."

He glanced at her and then straight ahead. "I think Vanessa went back to work because she couldn't stand being with a child all day. Even on weekends, she coaxed me to go out with her at least one night. But it was sort of a tug-of-war because I just liked being at home with my daughter."

What was Gabe trying to tell her? That Vanessa wasn't always the doting mother? "Tell me something, Gabe. Do you think Vanessa should have stayed home with Stephie instead of returning to work?"

After looking pensive for a moment, he kept walking. "I think that the ideal situation is for a mother to stay home with her child, especially the first few years. But I also understand that some women don't think that's enough. They want the stimulation of the working world. Vanessa was like that."

April decided to tell Gabe what she thought. "I think, if I ever had children, I'd *want* to stay home with them."

April's words hung in the cool, crisp air, and Gabe focused his attention on her, not averting his gaze for a long time. But finally he did. His gray-and-blue wool shirt jacket emphasized the broadness of his shoulders and the length of his long arms. She remembered being held in those arms, and longed to feel his embrace again.

They stood by the reservoir for a few moments in silence, watching the water bubble quietly by.

"I owe you an apology," Gabe said.

When April looked up at him, her heart beat faster. "For what?"

"For what I said to you Saturday night. For making you feel as if you were an experiment. When I kissed you, April, I wanted to kiss you—both times— just like I want to kiss you now."

It was time to take a risk and reach for what she wanted. "What's stopping you?" April asked softly, holding her breath.

"At this moment, nothing," Gabe replied as he clasped her shoulders and drew her gently toward him.

As he bent his head to her, the cool air seemed to evaporate. All she could feel was the heat of him, the longing to be closer, the need to have his lips on hers. His lips were warm on hers, firm, seductive. Then he slanted his mouth over hers and coaxed her lips apart. She didn't need much coaxing. When he thrust inside, he pressed her to him. Their jackets were impediments, and needing to touch him, she reached up and laced her fingers in his hair. When he groaned, a quiver ran through her, and the deepest center of her yearned for a physical joining. Melting into him, her hips met his, and a primal energy seemed to pull them tighter together. Gabe's hands slid down her back to cup her bottom, and she could feel his arousal, hard and hot, against her softness. The hungry thrusts of his tongue aroused passion that she'd ignored and denied and feared.

She loved Gabe's scent. She loved the calluses on his hands. She loved the way she felt when she was with him—safe and protected, yet excited. She responded to him by stroking over his tongue and pushing into his mouth, taking passion as well as giving it, letting him know this kiss was everything she wanted, too.

But her fervent response apparently didn't show Gabe how much she wanted him because he broke the kiss and stared down at her, his green eyes turbulent. "What are we doing, April?"

She tried to steady her breathing and her pulse. "I think that's obvious."

"Vanessa's only been gone less than a year. You're flying back to Boston in a few weeks. In spite of what I said the other night, I could never emulate Nicholas' lifestyle. I'm not the type of man to have affairs. But maybe you're the type of woman who wants them.

Are you?"

The turmoil inside Gabe was obvious from his expression, and she didn't know if he was lashing out because he felt guilty for taking pleasure from a woman other than his wife or because she had hurt him in the past and he didn't want to be hurt again. She couldn't blame him from wanting to stay away from her, for not wanting to feel the attraction between them. If she told him everything she was feeling in her heart, he might not believe her. If she told him about Stephie—

Stephie anchored Gabe's world. That was obvious. April couldn't divulge what she knew in an emotional moment or a passionate one or because she wanted Gabe to think less of Vanessa. Their situation was so tangled, she wasn't sure she could ever unravel it. But she was sure that this wasn't the time or the place, and she should pull her dignity around her however she could in order to keep living in Gabe's house.

"Do you want me to leave, Gabe?"

He raked his hand through his hair, and he seemed to be debating with himself. "Stephie needs you, and you certainly made life easier for me lately. But as I told you before, I don't want to take advantage of you, April, not in any way. So the choice is yours."

"I like taking care of Stephie. I told you that. Do you have any leads for nannies?"

Nodding, he said, "Two. I'm going to call them tomorrow morning."

"All right. After you decide whether they're suitable or not, then we'll go from there."

"April, I didn't plan to bring you here today to—"

"I know you didn't." This attraction between them just seemed to have a life of its own, and it flared up when they least expected it. She'd just have to be more careful until she was ready to tell Gabe everything—the truth about how she felt about him as well as the truth about Stephie.

Chapter Six

On Sunday, Gabe washed and waxed the cars while April sat in the living room by the smoldering fire reading the paper. Stephie was taking a nap, and she'd offered to help him. But he'd shaken his head and told her to take some time for herself for a change. She'd caught him looking at her throughout the day as if he was trying to figure her out.

When the phone rang, she put the paper aside and reached for it.

"April, it's your mother."

"Mother, how are you?"

"I'm just fine. I'm going to come to Cedar Corners for a visit before winter sets in. Clarice Barlow asked me to come stay with her for a while."

Clarice was one of her mother's friends from the garden club. A widow, she spent most of her time traveling or heading up the social events in Cedar Corners. "Why stay with Mrs. Barlow? You could come here."

"Oh, I don't want to crowd you and Gabe. Besides, I think Clarice is lonely. That's why she travels as much as she does. And I've missed her since I moved to Cocoa Beach. She and I will have a good time visiting. But I want to spend time with you and Stephie, too."

"When are you arriving?"

"Tomorrow afternoon."

"I'll pick you up at the airport."

"You don't have to do that. I'm going to rent a car. I'll get settled in with Clarice, then maybe I can come over in the evening."

"Come for supper."

"You're sure that won't be too much bother?"

"Mother, it's no bother cooking for one more person."

"So Gabe hasn't found anyone to keep house and take care of Stephie?"

"Not yet. But I'm enjoying it."

"I imagined you would," Winnifred said,

surprising April.

"What do you mean, Mother?"

"Oh, nothing. Vanessa was more like me. She preferred having a cook and a maid, but you—you like doing for others." Before April could question her mother further, Winnifred said, "So I'll give you a call after I get in tomorrow."

When April hung up the phone, she thought about what her mother had said. She didn't know if she enjoyed doing for others, but she certainly enjoyed taking care of Gabe and Stephie. But that was because she loved them.

Would her mother understand April's feelings towards Gabe? Could she confide Vanessa's secret in Winnifred? No. She couldn't confide what she knew to anyone.

April had to tell Gabe. But the time had to be right, and it wasn't yet. She would tell him soon.

****

April handed her mom an apron with a high bib top. "You'd better put this on."

April and her mother had never been what some people would term close, and there were many reasons for that. But since her sister had died, they seemed to understand each other a little better, could talk a little more, saw each day as a gift that had to be taken advantage of. Yet her mother was still her mother, always dressed beautifully and perfectly, as if she were stepping out to a very important occasion, even if she was just making supper with April, and Stephie, and Gabe. Well, Gabe wouldn't be making supper, but hopefully he would be enjoying it with them. Right now her mother's sunny yellow blouse and slacks could easily be marred by a splash of chicken broth, a swipe of flour, or Stephie's sticky hand as she helped make dumplings.

"You worry too much," Winnifred said. "I can always send it to the dry cleaners." But she swept the apron over her head and then tied the skirt at the waist.

"There's Daddy," Stephie said, pointing out the window as she saw her father carrying bush trimmings to the side of the garage. "I want to go with him."

"Instead of cooking with us?" Winnifred asked with a smile.

Stephie eagerly bobbed her head up and down.

"You can go out with your dad," Winnifred said, "but you have to wash your hands first. Come here,

I'll help." Winnifred bent to Stephie and lifted her up, sitting her on the counter. Then she turned on the spigot, grabbed a few paper towels, and helped her granddaughter wash her hands under the spigot, afterward drying them for her.

After she set Stephie on the floor, she took the little girl's jacket from the peg on the wall, and helped her into it. Then she went to the door and called to Gabe. "Stephie wants to come out with you. Is that okay?"

He looked at the pile of trimmings, then back at the other bushes that he hadn't done yet. "Sure, send her out. We'll play hide and seek and have a game of tag."

As soon as Winnifred opened the door, Stephie ran outside and over to her dad's arms.

Winnifred stood at the storm door. "She adores him."

April studied her mother carefully. Did she have any inkling of what Vanessa had done? Or what she'd confided?

"And Gabe loves her."

Should she tell her mother about Vanessa? Ask her opinion on what to do?

No, April had already made up her mind what she

had to do. She just didn't know when she was going to do it. Telling Gabe the truth was probably the hardest conversation they'd ever have.

"Can I ask you a question without you getting all upset?" April wanted to know.

"I suppose that depends on the question. I'll tell you up front if you think it's going to upset me, it probably will."

Her mother was right about that. "Why did you ignore Dad's affairs?"

As a teenager when her parents split, April had heard and seen things that made her understand what kind of marriage her parents had. The same had been true for Vanessa. They'd both known their dad had come home too late to be out at a business meeting. They both had smelled perfume other than what their mother wore when they hugged him. They'd both been aware that although their mom had a closet full of the prettiest clothes, the latest trends in shoes, the snazziest car, underneath it all, she hadn't been happy.

"You want a simple explanation when there isn't one. I divorced your father because of his affair."

"But that wasn't the first one. Vanessa and I both knew that. Did you really think we didn't notice what went on between the two of you?"

Winnifred still stared out the door without turning to look at April. "How many affairs do you think he had?"

"Oh, Mom, I didn't count. But I knew when he bought a new suit and changed his cologne, and had a certain look in his eye, that something was different. But if I had to guess, I'd say a half dozen."

Now Winnifred did turn to look at her. "So you and Vanessa were really that aware."

"We were. Why did you just ignore it?"

"There's something you have to understand about marriage, April. It changes constantly. One day, you can believe you have a perfect marriage. The next day, your husband looks at another woman as if he wants to be sleeping with her. I do believe men think it's all about the excitement in bed, not about living with someone day to day."

"You don't think they cross over?" April thought about Vanessa and why she might have cheated on Gabe. Just why would a woman do that? She suddenly had another thought. "Did you cheat on Dad?"

Winnifred instantly shook her head. "No, I don't have it in me. Unfortunately, I'm a one-man woman. Your father always came back to me, and sometimes it was better than before he had the latest affair."

"Mother."

"What, April? I'm just being realistic. We had a good life. I had every material possession I could want. More importantly, you and Vanessa did, too. A mother has to think about those things. A mother has to think about what's best for her children."

"Financial security is one thing. Emotional security is another. Do you think Vanessa and I couldn't see that you were unhappy?"

"I thought I put up a very good front."

"Because you had lunch with friends at the country club? Because you played golf and sat around the pool sipping drinks and went to lots of parties? That's not the same as being happy, and Vanessa and I knew that."

"Well, I wasn't going to sit around and mope. I wasn't going to try to change something I couldn't. I wasn't going to date a hundred more men looking for the right one, knowing there never was going to be one."

"Mother," April said again.

"Reality, April. Do you think there's a Mr. Right for you?"

Gabe instantly came to mind. "I hope so."

"He'll only be Mr. Right if you can be Miss Right, and then Mrs. Right. Obviously your father and I had different values. Did I know that when I married him? No, I was stupidly naïve. But then I made the best of a bad situation. Isn't that what life's all about?"

April suddenly felt weary. She shook her head. "Sometimes I don't know what life's all about."

If her sister had remained faithful, would she have been in that accident? If her sister had been Miss Right, and then Mrs. Right for Gabe, would they have been happy? Did Gabe still long for Vanessa, or had he realized something had been wrong with their marriage? Something had to be wrong with the marriage for Vanessa to stray. Didn't it?

In that pause, when so many thoughts and questions were clicking through her head, one question stood out to ask her mother. "So why did you finally divorce Dad?"

"I divorced him because he got involved with someone, and I knew the relationship was more than a fling." Her father had married a year after the divorce, but that had only lasted about three years.

"You thought he'd met Miss Right?"

Her mother shrugged. "With the others, he hadn't been emotionally absent with me. With the others, I knew the affairs would end. When he got involved with Lana, he acted different. When I talked to him, he wasn't there. He was thinking about her. When we went to a cocktail party, I knew he was wishing she was by his side, not me. It was different, and it was the kind of different I could no longer handle. He'd already put aside money for your college fund and Vanessa's. Vanessa was ready to graduate from high school, and you'd be graduating the following year. The house was paid for. I knew he'd settle enough money on me so I'd be comfortable the rest of my life if I invested it wisely, and I knew how because I'd handled a good part of our finances. The truth was, I had dirt on him. He confided in me about work. I knew secrets he wouldn't want let out about the inner workings of his law practice. So I asked him for the divorce and a settlement and told him what I'd do if he wouldn't give it to me."

April had never guessed her mother could be so calculating.

Because of this conversation, all the puzzle pieces fell into place for April. Her parents' relationship, her parents' marriage had instilled in her a basic lack of faith in the institution. The idea of marriage was scary to her because she'd built up a different view than what her parents had. A marriage wasn't supposed to be full of lies and looking the other way. It was supposed to be full of love and trust. She'd been confused by the concept, wanting one thing, seeing another. The idea of loving Gabe and trusting Gabe had just seemed too foreign, totally out of her realm of understanding or experience.

And now? Now she felt something with Gabe that was stronger than her doubts. She felt something with Gabe that led her to think she could be his Miss Right. Unlike Vanessa, she knew how to make a promise and stay loyal and faithful. Unlike Vanessa, she believed in vows. Unlike Vanessa, she'd love Gabe forever.

Love Gabe. Her knees felt weak at the thought. Still, she *did* love him. Because she did, she wanted to protect him. However, protecting him from the truth wasn't protection at all.

She asked her mother. "Are you happy now?"

Winnifred went to the stove, lifted the lid from pot of simmering chicken, and put it back on again. "I like to travel, and I can afford to do that a couple of times a year. And," she paused and cut a sideways glance at April before she stirred the dumpling mixture in the bowl. "And…I'm seeing someone. It's early days yet, but my heart does go pitty-pat whenever I'm with him."

"Pitty-pat?" April asked with a grin.

"You know what I mean."

"Are you going to let me meet him?"

"I want to give it a little more time, to see if it's going anywhere. Do you know what I mean?"

She did know exactly what her mother meant.

Were she and Gabe going anywhere?

Only time would tell.

"Come on," she said, "Let's get these dumplings going or we'll never get supper out."

Winnifred suddenly looked April squarely in the eyes. "You like being here with Gabe and Stephie, don't you?"

She could only tell her mother the truth. "Yes."

Winnifred nodded. "I thought so. But be careful, Honey. These are deep waters you're trying to swim in."

"I know."

Winnifred reached out and gave her a hug. "Maybe you'll have better luck than I did."

But April wasn't sure luck had anything to do with it at all.

****

Later that evening, Gabe walked Winnifred to her rental car parked in his driveway. Never at a loss for something to say, over dinner she'd told him about her life in Florida…the cruise she was going to take next. He'd made comments at the appropriate places.

He opened her car door for her.

She asked, "How would you feel if I moved back here again?"

Remembering conversation over dinner, he responded, "You sound like you're happy in Florida."

"I am, but— It would be nice to watch Stephie grow up."

Winnifred had never seemed to like messy babies. Maybe now that Stephie was growing older, she could relate to her better. She'd certainly seemed to today. She was an odd mix of both Vanessa and April. Like Vanessa, she was always pristinely dressed, her hair in place, her nails manicured. She liked nice things and wasn't ashamed of that fact. However, like April, she had a warmth about her when she spoke of her friends, when she showed she cared about Stephie by sending cards and presents, and today, reading to her in front of the fire. She was a complicated woman, but then, he supposed, what woman wasn't.

He wasn't sure exactly what to say, so he went with something easy. "If you moved back here, I think Stephie would appreciate having you here. The more people in her life who love her, the better."

Winnifred nodded at that and settled in the car's driver seat. Her hand on the seat belt, she said, "Clarice and I will be visiting an old friend in Leesburg tomorrow, but I'll be in touch when I get back." Then she closed the door and started the car.

He waited until she'd backed out of the driveway and headed for Clarice Barlow's.

After Gabe went into the house, he wondered if April was already putting Stephie to bed. But he found them in the living room, and the tableau made him stop and just stand there, studying April and Stephie. They were sitting on the floor in front of the fire. Rather April was sitting. Stephie was laying on the floor, her head in April's lap. April was brushing her hair and Stephie's eyes were closed. Neither of them knew he was there, or sensed he was there.

He didn't make a sound.

He studied Stephie's little face, then he studied April's profile. Aunt and niece were very different. They didn't look alike at all. Stephie still didn't resemble either him or Vanessa, either. He remembered seeing photos in one of the albums of April and Vanessa when they were kids. Stephie didn't look like either of them had in those early pictures. Maybe she was just a conglomeration of them all.

"It looks as if someone is past ready for pajamas and brushing her teeth," he said.

April jumped. His voice had startled her. Apparently she'd been deep in thought as she brushed his daughter's hair. "She had a full day and no nap. Mother used to brush my hair and Vanessa's."

"She didn't leave that to the nanny?"

"No. She always put us to bed herself, at least as often as she could. Sometimes she and Dad would go to parties, and then Cora would attend to us. But she liked reading us stories, too. It brought back memories to see her reading to Stephie tonight."

It seemed April was in an introspective and reflective mood. "Do you and your mother talk about Vanessa?"

"Sometimes we do. Today we didn't. Why?"

"Winnifred asked me what I thought about her moving back here. Did she tell you she was thinking about it?"

"No, she didn't. Matter of fact, she told me she was seeing someone. If she moved back here, I wonder what would happen with that."

"Maybe she's afraid to stay there and find out what could happen." The words were out of his mouth before he thought better of it. He shouldn't have said that.

April's cheeks pinkened. "Maybe that's so."

Five years ago, Gabe's pride had kept him from asking April to stay. What if he convinced her staying was better than leaving? What if he let those old feelings resurface?

"April, I didn't say that because—" He stopped.

"Because that's what I did? I wish we could leave the past in the past, don't you?"

"I doubt if that's possible."

April set down the brush, but she tenderly pushed Stephie's hair away from her forehead.

Before April could take his daughter into her arms to carry her up to bed, something made him ask, "Did you know any of Vanessa's colleagues?"

April blinked at the sudden change of subject. "Her colleagues?" She frowned, and she bit her lower lip. She only did that when she was nervous. What would she be nervous about?

But then she lifted her head and looked at him squarely. "No, I never met any of Vanessa's colleagues. Why?"

Gabe shrugged, not wanting his suspicions about not being Stephie's father tormenting him again. He'd been so overjoyed when Stephie was born that he hadn't questioned her full-term weight when she was born three weeks early. Now he seemed to be questioning everything.

He approached April and Stephie, and sat on the edge of the sofa. "No reason, really. I was just looking through some old pictures. I realized how little I knew about Vanessa's work life. How little I knew about so many things."

"You can only know if the other person's willing to tell you," April said softly.

Now exactly what did that mean? Gabe wondered. Was she trying to say that two people in a relationship had to be totally honorable and totally open? That was asking for the moon.

"Tell me something, Gabe. What are your dreams for the future?"

He could feel his guard going up because he suspected the question was a lead-in to something else. "I don't dream any more. I deal with reality. My main goal is to raise Stephie to be a happy person with strong values."

"So you have dreams for her, but not for yourself?"

"That's about right."

April seemed disappointed at his answer. After a few moments, she put her arms around Stephie and whispered to her, "Come on, little one, time to go to bed."

But Gabe was off the sofa and lifting Stephie into his own arms. "I'll carry her up," he said.

As he mounted the stairs, he realized the one reality he might have to face—the possibility he wasn't Stephie's father. He remembered a conversation between the nurses the night of the accident. They'd been discussing Larry Powell. He'd overheard one say to the other that the man had no relatives to notify. How had they known that? Had Vanessa managed to tell them that before she died? Just how well had she known Larry Powell?

So many questions.

But Gabe wasn't sure he wanted to know the answers.

Chapter Seven

April asked Gabe if he wanted to go along to buy Stephie new winter clothes on Saturday, and to her surprise he agreed. Maybe he wanted to go along to make sure she didn't go over budget…or she didn't overspend…or she didn't go overboard. But he bought everything she picked up from the faux fur winter coat in an animal print pattern to the cute little boots with pompoms, from the denim coveralls to the pink blouse with the ruffle around the neck, to the bumblebee Halloween costume for the kids' party at the fire company's social hall next weekend. It was easy to see he wouldn't deny his daughter anything.

Even if she wasn't his daughter?

One of April's major concerns on whether or not

she should tell Gabe the truth was Stephie. What would telling him do to his relationship with his daughter? Because she *was* his daughter in every way that mattered.

Home from their excursion, Gabe parked in the driveway, opened the back door and unhitched Stephie from her car seat while April gathered up some of the packages.

April was helping Stephie out of her jacket in the living room when Gabe said, "I'll take all the bags upstairs. I'm going to change into some old clothes so I can finish the yard work."

April was no sooner in the kitchen with Stephie, finding an apple in the refrigerator to cut up for a snack for her, when the doorbell rang. Knowing Gabe was upstairs, she didn't hesitate to answer it. When she opened it, she found Debra Evans, the single mom from the preschool open house. She was taken aback when she saw April, but then her smile resurfaced. She was carrying a plate of something covered with aluminum foil.

Gabe was coming down the steps by then, and Stephie had run to the door, too.

Since it was obvious this woman was here to see Gabe, April stepped aside. Debra's little girl was beside her and he smiled down at her as he said, "This is a surprise."

The woman frowned. "I left a message on your answering machine. I told you I'd stop by around two with some brownies for a play date and you should call me if there was a problem, otherwise I'd just show up. So here I am."

Gabe looked at April, but she just shook her head. She hadn't checked the machine.

"We were out all morning, so I missed you message." Then politely, he said, "But I'm sure Stephie would like to play with Beverly. Come on in. Brownies are always welcome."

Brownies are always welcome? April thought.

Debra took the cover from the brownies and held them up to Gabe's nose to take a whiff. "Isn't chocolate the best aphrodisiac?"

Gabe didn't seem comfortable with that idea, and he glanced down at the girls. "Stephie, why don't you get out a game for the two of you to play? Or dolls…or something."

"Toy box," Stephie said gleefully, and went to the corner of the living room where it was kept. Debra's little girl followed her.

"How about some coffee to go with this?" Gabe

asked amiably, as if the idea of coffee and brownies might be a good thing. "We had an early lunch to go shopping, so I'm sure we're all ready for a snack." He looked to April for confirmation of that fact.

She wasn't confirming anything. She felt like a third wheel. This was no place for her right now. Not with the flirting that was going to go on.

"I'm going to go for a jog," she explained. Then she nodded to the plate. "Maybe I'll have one of those later after I earned it."

Debra looked pleased. Gabe? She wasn't sure if he liked Debra's attention and the idea of a chocolate aphrodisiac or not.

She couldn't tell what Gabe was feeling, so she ran up the stairs to change her clothes. Apparently Gabe's yard work could wait until after brownies and coffee. April knew she was going to go for a very *long* jog.

****

When April returned down the stairs, Stephie and Beverly were sprawled on the floor in the living room, dolls and their clothes spread around them. She heard the low voices of Gabe and Debra in the kitchen. After a smile for the girls and a wave good-bye, she hurried outside.

Once on the front lawn, April stretched. Five minutes later, she started out at a walk, then a fast walk, then a jog, then a run. She felt as if she wanted to outrun every thought and feeling. This morning, she and Gabe had been buying clothes for Stephie. Innocuous enough, right?

Sure, until their hands brushed when they felt the fabric…until their elbows hit each other when they pulled a coat off a rack…until their gazes met and they remembered kisses from both now and in the past. They'd accomplished their goal—fitting Stephie with a winter wardrobe. Yet under the surface was a constant tension…under the surface was a knowledge they wanted each other…under the surface was the fact that they were both holding back.

April jogged often but she was usually focused, intent on where she was going, completely aware of everything around her and in front of her. Today, however, she was distracted. She felt the leaves under her running shoes. She knew they moved, some of them still slick from another rain earlier in the week. But she'd run on all surfaces. She'd splashed through puddles. She'd even jogged on ice.

The sun was bright today as she ran to the corner.

It flashed off of the windshield of a parked car, practically blinding her. However, she didn't slow down. She couldn't. She didn't want to.

That was when it happened.

Her right foot slipped. Her feet felt like they were sliding out from under her, and she fell hard on her left knee. She'd worn her jogging shorts because she'd been in a hurry. Even though she'd grabbed her warm-up jacket, her legs were bare. She was breathing hard from the run, trying to absorb what had happened in the fall, gasping for breath she couldn't seem to find. She closed her eyes and calmed herself, told herself all she had to do was breath. But pain was shooting up her leg, and she felt the brushburns and scrapes below her knee. Finally opening her eyes, she looked at her leg. Dirty and ugly-looking, she knew she was going to have bruises as well as scrapes and brushburns.

Her jog had ended. It might have ended for the next week or so. That depended on if anything else hurt.

She slowly rose to her feet, expecting pain in her knee. It ached a little, but surprisingly, it wasn't bad. Fortunately, for the most part, her leg had taken the brunt of it. It felt as if it was on fire and hurt like the dickens. Since she had jogged about a mile from Gabe's house, this was going to be a long walk home.

****

Gabe had said good-bye to Debra as soon as it was feasible to do so. Fortunately Stephie had given him the perfect out. She and Beverly had squabbled over something and Stephie had begun crying. Without a nap, she'd gotten over-tired. He'd told Debra they'd have to cut the playdate short today.

He'd just come downstairs after settling Stephie in her room, when he saw April limping up the front path to the door. He didn't think twice about rushing to the door and opening it for her.

When he saw her leg, he felt his jaw tighten, but he managed to unclench it. "What happened?"

"What does it look like?" she asked, limping to the chair and holding onto the arm before she sat.

"It looks like you took a pretty bad fall. You've got to get that cleaned up."

"I just walked a mile after the fall, so give me a minute, okay?"

He was handling this all wrong. He'd always handled April all wrong. Maybe it was because he felt too much when he was around her. Maybe it was because he'd always wondered what they could have had. Maybe it was because he'd committed himself to another woman and hadn't wanted to regret it.

"Did you hurt your knee?"

"I think the knee's okay, maybe just bruised a little."

"I'll be right back," he muttered, going into the kitchen.

He kept an ice bag in the freezer for basketball strains and, once in a while, Stephie's boo-boos. He grabbed that, wrapped it in a towel and poured a glass of orange juice. Then he took both into April. After handing her the orange juice, he gently laid the ice bag on her knee. She sighed and looked up at him with wide brown eyes. "Thank you."

Her voice sounded a little thick and he suspected the pain was getting to her.

"Why didn't you phone me?"

"Because I didn't have my cell phone along."

"That's because you shot out of here like a rabbit with a hunter after it."

"Don't be silly. I just wanted to get out of your way."

At that he shook his head. "You weren't in my

way. In fact, if you'd been here, the whole scenario would have been a lot more comfortable."

"I wasn't going to sit here and watch you flirt with her in front of me."

"April." Her name was a scolding warning.

"Tell me she didn't flirt with you, and you didn't flirt back."

"I didn't flirt back." He enunciated each word so she'd get his drift.

"She wants to go out with you."

"Tell me something I don't know. I didn't invite her here today, April. She invited herself. So I don't know why you're angry at *me*."

"I'm not angry at you."

He hiked up his brows.

She shook her head. "Oh, Gabe, everything between us is always so complicated."

She was definitely right about that. There was silence for a little while as she finished the juice.

But once she did, he said, "You really need to get this leg cleaned up. I'll carry you upstairs."

"You will not. Can't I just bandage it down here?"

"I ran out of antiseptic down here, and the antibacterial soap is upstairs, too. My bathroom. Come on, let's get this done."

"You're bossy," she murmured.

"No, I'm the best part of your good sense. It's telling you what you should do."

A cloud seemed to cross April's face and he wondered if she suddenly felt a jolt of pain.

"I have ibuprofen upstairs, too," he cajoled.

"Blackmail."

"Whatever works."

April had a stubborn streak and he knew he had to get past that. He also had to get past her sense of independence and her resolution that she didn't need anyone else.

When he took the ice pack from her knee, April stood. "It feels better already."

"That's just because it's numb. If you won't let me help, take your time on the stairs."

When she didn't reply to that, it took everything in him not to sweep her up into his arms and carry her up there. But he didn't. He did stand by, though, just in case her knee buckled, just in case the pain took her down.

Walking beside her until she reached the stairs, he stood behind her, making sure she could handle what she was trying to do. He knew she hurt. He knew the stairs weren't easy. He knew she wouldn't complain.

But he did see her wince with each step, and each of those winces hurt him.

At the top she was breathing heavy but he could see she was glad she'd made it without his assistance. That was April.

She took off her warm-up jacket though because the exertion had obviously overheated her. He took it from her and she didn't protest.

"I guess Stephie's taking a nap?" she almost whispered as they walked down the hall.

As they went by April's bedroom, he tossed her jacket inside over the chair then rejoined her. "She and Beverly had a little tiff and she started crying so it was a good excuse to ask Debra to leave. I told her I had to put Stephie down for a nap."

"You asked her to leave?"

He stopped in the middle of the hall and took April by the shoulders. "You're one exasperating woman. I didn't want her here in the first place."

April had the grace to look embarrassed. "Okay, I'm sorry."

"There's nothing to be sorry about. You just had a parallel reaction to how I felt about Nicholas."

To his surprise, April didn't protest. She didn't contradict him and say she wasn't jealous. Maybe that was progress. Maybe they were finally being honest with each other.

As they walked through his bedroom to the bathroom, he spied April looking around. When her gaze fell on the photo of him and Vanessa and Stephie that was on his dresser, she looked away. Too difficult to think about Vanessa's death? Too difficult to think about him and Vanessa and Stephie as a family? Too difficult to think about their kisses, what they'd shared and what she'd given up?

Maybe later he'd get the answers to those questions and others, too.

At his bathroom, he went in ahead of her, pulled the black enamel bench away from the vanity and pointed to it.

But, of course, she protested. "If you just get everything out, I can do it myself."

"I'll get everything out, but I'll do it to make sure you've cleaned the scrapes well. Believe me, if you do it yourself, it will hurt more."

"You know this from experience?"

"I've had sports injuries."

"Recently?"

"Nicholas and I go at it pretty hard sometimes. I've ended up in the emergency room on occasion and so has he."

"Bonding time," she said with a straight face.

He chuckled. "Women go shopping. Men play sports."

"Some women go shopping. Others…have lunch, watch a movie, or just share a glass of wine."

He turned to the long, floor to ceiling cabinet beside the shower. "Do you have good friends in Boston?"

Supplies in his hands when he turned around, he saw her watching him. He put everything on the sink and turned on the spigot.

"Yes, I have good friends, some married, some not. Charlene and Emma are probably my best friends. Charlene is married. Emma isn't. Why are you asking?"

"Because I really don't know much about your life, and because— I don't think Vanessa had friends she could confide in. She worked a lot of hours and that didn't leave much time for friendships, I guess."

"That's silly, Gabe. There's always time for friends."

He shrugged. "She liked parties. You know that. It seemed she liked to be with groups of people rather than with one or two at a time. Wouldn't you say that was true?"

April looked away for a moment, and then she shrugged. "Yes, I think that was true. She was a party girl."

Gabe put his knuckle under her chin and lifted her face so she'd meet his eyes. "And you're not?"

"No, I'm not."

Taking a clean washcloth, he ran it under warm water, wrung it out, then laid it gently over the worst of April's scrapes and cuts.

"That hurts," she murmured.

"I know, but it will help prepare you for what comes next."

"You're going to give me a bullet to bite on?"

"I can give you a towel to bite. This isn't going to be pleasant. Not when I scrub it."

"Just do it. Let's get it over with."

So they did. But when Gabe was finished with the warm water and the soap, with the rinsing and the antiseptic and the bandaging, April was pale.

"You're not going to pass out on me, are you?"

"No," she snapped, then in a gentler voice, she added, "But I do think I'll lie on my bed for a while. That is, if you don't need me for anything else."

Need her for something else. Oh, yes, he did. His

bathroom wasn't too small, but it wasn't large, either. Being this close to her, touching her as he had, taking care of her had easily aroused him. April easily aroused him. He'd fought old feelings for her up until this visit. He'd fought the chemistry between them up until this visit. Now, he wanted to give into it and see where it took them. But he wasn't going to take advantage of this situation. He wouldn't take advantage of April while she was hurting.

She stood and gingerly took a step forward. He could tell by the expression on her face that her leg certainly didn't feel better.

"I'll get that ibuprofen," he muttered.

****

It was almost two a.m. when Gabe finally gave up the battle of tossing and turning and trying to go to sleep. His mind just wouldn't shut down. His evening with April and Stephie had been spent quietly. Fortunately, they'd had left-overs for supper so food preparation hadn't been a big deal. He'd insisted on cleaning up and April hadn't argued. That was a first. Afterward, they'd played board games with Stephie and put puzzles together. That way, April didn't have to move around so much. He'd caught a grateful glance more than once. Those grateful glances did funny things to his heart rate. Either that, or he'd had too much caffeine at supper.

Sure, blame it on the caffeine.

He threw off the covers and stood by the side of the bed. Those brownies Debra had brought over were still downstairs. One of them probably wasn't much better than another cup of coffee, but at least he'd enjoy it, at least he wouldn't be thinking about April not so far down the hall lying alone in her bed.

However, once downstairs, he thought about April upstairs. The brownie tasted dry in his mouth and chocolate didn't seem a solution to anything. Maybe he'd just go back upstairs and read until he fell asleep.

He'd left the light on in his bedroom, but hadn't turned on the hall lamp. He knew every inch of this house by heart. Ambient light from the moon shone through the skylight in the hall. He was just climbing the stairs when the door to April's room opened and she stepped into the hall. She was wearing a pale pink nightgown that stopped halfway down her thighs. It was silky with little cap sleeves and a boat neck. It slid to one side now.

He heard a small gasp when she saw him.

"Gabe."

"Can't sleep?" he asked, his voice husky. "Do you need more ice? I'll go get it."

"No, no more ice. It hurts. I'm restless. When I turn over, my leg brushes the sheets."

"Tomorrow I'll get some of those patches with the antibiotic right on the patch. It will be easier for you to change the dressing."

"I was just going to get a glass of water."

But she wasn't moving toward the bathroom. She was standing perfectly still, staring at him. Well, staring at his chest that was bare. He could practically feel her eyes passing down his chest, straight down the middle, down to the low ride of his jogging shorts, further—

She saw immediately what her perusal had done and her gaze slipped back up to his. Denying anything would be stupid. He wasn't going to deny this attraction to her, not anymore. He climbed the remaining few steps and approached her.

"What do you need, April? Someone to sing you a lullaby?"

"I don't need anything. I'll just grab another pill."

He clasped her elbow. "Do you think a pill is going to help?"

They were speaking in implied words and underlying messages. It was time they got plain about it. "I can give you something to take your mind off the pain."

"Something more than ibuprofen?"

"Not a controlled substance. Something much better, though I've heard kissing can be addictive."

He leaned toward her and bent his head. There was no doubt as to what he was going to do. She could have backed away. She could have said no. She could have put her hands against his chest so their bodies wouldn't touch. But she didn't do any of those things. She just stood there and waited.

That was the loudest and most graphic signal. Her acquiescence told him she wanted his kiss. When her arms banded around him, he brought her tighter against him. She lifted her lips to his and he took advantage of the invitation. This kiss wasn't going to be hurried or quick. This kiss was going to tell him things he wanted to know. This kiss was going to answer some of the questions he had.

This kiss.

He knew his arms were possessive. He knew his mouth was claiming. He knew his tongue was seductive. Everything about this kiss was intent on seduction.

Although he was lost in kissing her, he was mindful of her leg and careful when he swept her up into his arms.

"Gabe," her voice held a question and a bit of wonder.

"I'm taking you to my room." The underlying message there was clear. "Speak now if you don't want me to."

She didn't say anything. She just held on as if she wanted this as much as he did.

The room wasn't very far away, yet it seemed like it was. "Are you hurting?"

"Not when you're kissing me," she teased.

Her flirty response almost made him groan. It was another assent that she wanted this as much as he did.

In his bedroom, he gently laid her on the bed, but she kept her arms around his neck as if she didn't want to let go. He knew the feeling. Now that they had physical contact, now that they knew they were going to do this, he didn't want to leave her for a moment.

Sitting beside her on the huge bed, he kissed her again and again and again. Finally they broke for air and April slid over. He quickly pulled off his shorts and joined her.

Turning to her, he ran his hand over the slinky fabric of her nightgown, caressing every curve underneath. Although he desperately wanted to join their bodies, he found he wanted intimacy with her almost as much.

"What happened when you fell today? Were you crossing the street?"

"Just running. Going too fast for the conditions."

"The pavement was dry."

"The leaves were wet," she reminded him.

"You're a focused runner," he said, remembering. "Where was your head?"

She went silent and he understood there was a reason she didn't want to tell him. Because it would reveal too much about what she'd been feeling? Or something else. Maybe she and Winnifred had had a disagreement.

"Did you and your mom fight?"

"We don't fight. We have unilateral discussions. But, no, nothing like that. In fact...during this visit, she's told me some things about her marriage that I'd never known."

"Like?" he prompted, thinking maybe this was the root of why April had fallen.

"It's not important."

He caressed her cheek and lifted her chin. "Don't lie to me."

"I'm not." Her denial was more vehement than it should have been, and he wondered what that was coming from. But he waited, not wanting to push her.

"Mother admitted Dad had had multiple affairs. That wasn't a secret. Vanessa and I both had known about a few of them. It wasn't the quantity that bothered me, it was the way Mother had thought about it. As long as it was just sex he was after, she could live with it. But when one of the affairs turned serious, then she couldn't. That's when she divorced him."

"That's kind of a perverted look at marriage, isn't it? Aren't sex and everyday life supposed to go together?" he asked, glimpsing a deeper look into April and Vanessa's backgrounds.

"That's essentially how I responded, and she said I was naïve. She said that mothers sometimes have to do what they have to do, for whatever's best for their kids. She felt staying, having an opulent roof over our heads, being able to pay for the best schools, the luxury of never having to worry about money, was best for all of us. I don't know, Gabe. Do men look at it the same way? Would a man stay together for finances? To keep his family from falling apart?"

But as soon as April asked the question, she looked as if she wished she hadn't.

"There are some women who wouldn't stay past one affair," he said. "Your mother's generation is different from ours. Their thoughts on the subject are different, too."

"But she took us to church every Sunday. We know vows are meant to be kept. Isn't black black? Isn't white white? Or do you mix it into gray to sort it into your own needs? I want to believe in more than everybody being selfish."

He took her hands, brought them into his chest, and kissed her knuckles. "Then do believe, and it will be. Isn't that how the saying goes?"

"If only that was true," she murmured, lowering her gaze from his.

Something seemed to be bothering her, but she wasn't ready to divulge what it was, let alone confide in him. But she would soon.

Because he was going to convince her to trust him.

He kissed her forehead and then her eyelids, and then her mouth. She made a little sigh and wrapped her arms around him.

"I don't want to hurt you," he said, thinking about her leg.

"I don't want to hurt *you*, either," she murmured, and he realized she'd taken what he said a different way.

How could they hurt each other by pleasuring each other? How could they hurt each other by just living in the now for a change? When was the last time he'd done that?

As he kissed her again, his hands bunched up the silky gown. He drew it up her body…up, up, up and over her head until there was no longer a barrier between them. Not the soft material one, anyway. Maybe soon there wouldn't be any others, either.

He'd fallen in love with April all those years ago, and now he felt as if it were happening all over again. His hands were possessive as he cupped her breasts. His mouth was greedy as he took everything she'd give.

He broke away and asked, "Does it hurt to bend your knee?"

"No," she told him. "I want you, Gabe. I want you more than I've ever wanted anything. When you kiss me, nothing else matters. When you touch me, I only feel where you touch me, nothing else."

"Are you on the pill?" he asked.

"No, because I haven't been involved with anyone. Because I never expected—"

"I stopped at the drugstore yesterday afternoon," he said. "I didn't plan for this to happen, but yet that last kiss—" He stopped.

She put a finger over his lips, telling him she didn't need an explanation. So he reached for the nightstand drawer, pulled it open, and found a condom.

They took their time, which was excruciatingly frustrating, but tantalizingly exciting. He caressed her until she was breathless. She touched him, rolled on the condom, and held him in her hand. He felt as if he were going to burst into a million pieces. Then he thought about the best way to make her comfortable. He lay on his side and he brought her good leg up over his hip.

He stroked her hair, kissed her lips, rubbed his beardline against her breasts until she said, "I can't take any more of this, Gabe. Please make love to me."

Love. Is that what they were doing? Is that what they had? Did it even matter?

He wrapped his arm around April and thrust into her body. Her moan of assent drove him on. She kissed his chest and stroked his back. When her hand dipped below his waist to his backside, he was gone. His last thrust pushed her over the edge, too, and she clung to him, shaking, reverberating with the climax that had taken their world and turned it upside down.

A few minutes later, when their breathing had returned to normal—or more normal than it had been—he was going to pull away. But April wouldn't let him. She held on tight.

"Do you really want to go?" she whispered.

The way he felt right now, he never wanted to be anywhere but here.

"No, I don't want to go, but at some point I'll have to. Stephie still calls out some nights in her sleep."

"If she does, we'll be here for her, right?"

There was something in April's eyes that he didn't understand, something that made her question that fact. But that couldn't be. She knew he loved his daughter, no matter what. But he felt as if he might have to find out the truth behind the "no matter what."

Tomorrow, he'd go back to doing that. Tomorrow, he'd also start showing April how much she meant to him…that maybe, just maybe, she could be his future.

Chapter Eight

As Gabe sat at his desk on Monday, he realized yesterday had been…a day more satisfying and pleasurable than he'd ever spent.

Because of April.

They'd awakened in each other's arms, taken Stephie to the Halloween party the Chamber of Commerce threw for kids at the fire company's social hall, spent the evening playing games with Stephie and then the night—

He couldn't even describe the night as they'd made love, fallen asleep, then reached for each other and done it again. He hadn't had time for breakfast this morning because he had an errand to run before work and they'd stayed in bed too long!

He'd managed to dress while April had made coffee and he'd taken a mug of it along after a kiss that reminded them of the night before. But that rushed morning "good-bye" led him to understand they needed even more time together. Tonight after Stephie went to bed would be the perfect opportunity to really talk about a subject they'd both avoided—the future.

However, nothing at all went the way Gabe had planned.

It all started with a mid-afternoon phone call from April.

"My mother phoned," she'd told him. "She wants me to go look at a condo with her tonight. She's trying to decide what she might want if she moves back here. I don't know what you were thinking about tonight—"

He'd been doing more than thinking about tonight. He'd been anticipating it with vivid pictures in his head. He'd planned to stop on the way home for strawberries and whipped cream. He'd planned to put Stephie to bed and then feed April those strawberries and give her the locket he'd bought for her this morning before he'd come to his office…the locket she'd so admired a few weeks ago. Nevertheless, he knew Winnifred would be leaving soon, and the time she and April spent together was important.

"My plans can change," he said. "Go with your mom and give her your advice."

"I doubt she'll take my advice."

"You never know. Don't hold back with her, April. Life's too short for that."

She paused as if his words had startled her. Then she responded, "You're right. Life *is* too short for that. I'll see you when you get home."

She sounded as if she were looking forward to that as much as he was.

Nevertheless, when he walked in his house, it seemed to be in total chaos. Burgers were patted, ready to broil but they were sitting on the counter. Salad fixings were spread from the mixer to the canisters. A frozen bag of broccoli lay haphazardly next to a pot.

When Gabe went into the living room, he saw Stephie's toys straggled from one end of it to the other. To top it all off, Stephie was sitting in a chair, crying. He supposed his daughter was experiencing a time-out. On her knees, April was picking up tiny pieces of paper that had been strewn all over the floor.

"Uh oh," Gabe said as he walked in. "What's this

mess?"

April glanced over her shoulder at him, and to her credit, she didn't erupt after what must have been a frustrating afternoon.

As soon as she saw him, Stephie popped up out of her chair and ran to him. He caught her and hugged her but said, "Hold on a minute. Are you supposed to be in time-out?"

She dropped her head and looked down at her sneakers. Then she nodded.

"How much longer?" he asked April.

"Two minutes. She just sat there a minute ago."

He tapped his watch. "Two minutes, kiddo."

Stephie started crying but he shook his head. "No crocodile tears. Come on." He patted the chair. "Two minutes. Just think about all the games we can play later, and it will go fast."

With a sullen look at both of them, Stephie dragged her feet walking to the chair and then plopped on it.

Gabe nodded to the kitchen, and April stepped that way with him, out of earshot of Stephie.

April shook her head. "I'm sorry the place is such a mess. She's just off today. Nothing satisfies her. Her attention span is zilch. She's just not her usual bubbly self. Maybe she's coming down with something."

"Fever? Stomach ache?"

April shook her head. "No, I checked. Nothing outward…yet. But I'm running late and dinner's not done, let alone the toys—"

Suddenly the doorbell rang. April examined her watch. "Oh, my gosh, it's Mother. I don't want to leave you with all this."

"All what? This is my life, April. This is nothing new. You've just made it a heck of a lot easier the past few weeks. But we're good. I can slide the burgers into the oven, cook a little broccoli, and even microwave a baked potato if I have to."

April smiled, and he realized how much he liked that smile, especially when it was just for him. "Go get the door, and tell your mom after you look at houses, she has to buy you something to eat."

"I'll grab a container of yogurt. I'll be fine."

"Stopping with your mom somewhere and having coffee and a sandwich could be good. You don't have to hurry back."

She eyed him briefly before she crossed to the door, and he wondered if he sounded a little too nonchalant. He wondered if he sounded as if he didn't care if they spent time together tonight. He gave himself a mental kick. He didn't know how to do this anymore.

Do what? a little voice inside his head asked.

Fall for someone, he answered under his breath. Then he corrected himself. *Fall for April, all over again.*

****

Two hours later, Gabe realized how right April had been when she'd said Stephie was "off." His daughter was cranky, contrary and argumentative. She'd gone through a stage like this when she was around two and had learned to say no. Tonight reminded him of that.

Finally, however, he coaxed her to eat a couple of bites of an overdone burger, convinced her a carrot stick was as good as candy, and told her if she helped him pick up her toys, she could have a cookie before bed. He'd picked up most of the toys, but …

She'd practically fallen asleep in the middle of one of the stories he'd read her. He gave her a kiss and was ready to go downstairs when he walked by the spare room next to April's. The door in there led up to the attic.

Maybe it was time he really put the past behind him. He still had a box up there that held a lot of Vanessa's papers as well as cards and mementoes from when they'd courted. He hadn't had the heart to go through them before. But now, maybe it was time.

This time of year, the attic was cool but not cold. Boxes with Christmas decorations lodged against one wall. A three-foot tall aluminum reindeer with lights guarded them.

Decorations for Christmas. He'd soon have to think about that. He'd soon have to think about asking April to stay. Would she consider staying permanently? Would she consider relocating?

Easily spotting the box he was concerned with— Vanessa's name in magic marker danced across the side—he crossed to it and pulled it away from under the eaves. Then he sat on the floor, ready to take everything to the paper shredder that reminded him of the past.

He wasn't sure how long he sorted. There were pay stubs and check stubs, cards they'd sent each other early in their courtship, but also e-mails Vanessa had printed out for one reason or the other—about a sale at a particular store, a few from long-distance friends, research for something for work. He found ticket stubs from a concert. He remembered the night he'd taken Vanessa to it, her excitement at hearing a band she loved. When he came to another batch of receipts, he glanced at them. Vanessa bought a lot of clothes, purses, shoes, jewelry. That was just the kind of woman she was.

There was one particular jewelry store that she liked the most. The receipt stated exactly the items beside each price—earrings, a necklace, two bracelets. But then his gaze fell on a receipt for an expensive men's watch.

He recognized the designer name. He'd never received a watch like that from Vanessa. Maybe, of course, it was work-related. Maybe everyone had gone together to give somebody a retirement gift. But now Gabe handled the receipts more carefully and looked more closely.

He heard noise downstairs.

Suddenly April called up the attic steps. "Gabe, are you up there?"

"Yes," he called back. "I'll just be a minute."

As he glanced at a few more receipts, he saw more women's items. Then he spotted another men's item—onyx and diamond cufflinks.

Maybe Vanessa was the social chairman at work

and bought gifts necessary for the company.

Maybe not.

Before he could even process the idea of Vanessa buying men's jewelry for someone other than him, April came up the stairs. He quickly changed thought channels. He purposely set the receipts back in the box on top of another stack of e-mails.

At a glance, April saw Vanessa's name on the box, as well as the papers he'd been sorting through. "What are you doing?"

"I thought it was time I emptied this last box. This is everything that had been in her desk at work and from her desk here. None of it seemed important after she died so I just stuffed it all up here."

"Is it important now?" April asked.

Was the fact that his wife had bought jewelry for other men important? He wasn't sure yet. Maybe he'd have to dig to the bottom of the box to find out. But he'd had enough for one night.

He didn't answer April's question, but rather asked, "So how did it go tonight?" Standing, he moved closer to her.

She glanced down at the papers again and then back at him. "Mother saw a condo she likes. She wouldn't have to worry about a yard or maintenance.

She could call someone if she had a leaky faucet. There's a reasonable monthly fee for all that. It seemed to be ideal."

"Seemed to be?"

"She still likes the idea of a small house of her own, so she's going to think about it."

"So she's serious about moving back here."

"I think so, though I don't know how that will affect her new dating relationship. Or if she cares if it does. I'm not sure she wants to *be* with anyone."

Gabe motioned to the stairs. "Let's go down."

"You don't want to put that back in the box?" she motioned to the papers.

"No. I'll come back up tomorrow night and finish. I've been putting it off for too long."

After they returned to the second floor, April asked, "So how was Stephie?"

"An armful. But she did fall asleep easily. It's possible she was just overtired."

"I suppose," April said.

"Did you eat?" he asked.

"We stopped at a family diner. I had a sandwich and mother had a cup of coffee."

Of one mind, they walked down the hall to Stephie's room. The door was ajar and they both peeked inside. She was sleeping peacefully on her side and looked like a little angel.

"To be able to sleep like that," April murmured.

Gabe nudged her around to face him. "You're not sleeping well?"

"I have a lot on my mind."

"Like?" he prompted.

She only hesitated a second. "Like…us."

She looked so vulnerable at that moment, as if the past two nights had been particularly special to her. He slid his hand under her hair, bent his head, brought her close, and claimed her lips. Her response was exactly what he'd hoped it would be—excited, passionate, and reciprocating.

He didn't hold back but pressed her against the wall. Their bodies fit together so well. Her hands had gone around his neck and now he took them from there and held one on either side of her head. She rubbed her breasts against his chest, teasing them both, and he muffled a groan.

"Do you know what you're doing?" he whispered.

"The same thing *you're* doing," was her flip reply.

He pressed another kiss to her lips while he matched their bodies and rocked his hips against hers.

When he broke away, she murmured, "Gabe, I'm

going to melt at your feet."

Is that what he wanted? April melting at his feet? What he wanted, was to make love to a woman knowing she was as enthralled with sex as he was, knowing giving and receiving pleasure was on both their minds, understanding that joining their bodies was more than physical. He'd tasted that exquisite pleasure with April and was hungry for it all over again.

He kissed April's eyelids, the curve of her cheek, the line of her neck. "My bedroom or yours?" he asked in a raspy tone.

"Gabe, maybe we should talk first. I have something I want to—"

"Talking is overrated," he decided, kissing her again. He wanted to make her breathless with need. He wanted their desire to unravel her and make her come apart in his arms.

Scooping her up, he carried her to his bedroom. Once there, he shut the door. By his bed, he laid April on it and looked down at her. He had to be sure about where they were headed. He had to be sure their desires matched. "Is this where you want to be?" he asked huskily.

She glanced at the bed and then up at him. "I want

to be with you."

That's all he needed to hear. "Undress," he said."

"You don't want to do it?" she asked playfully.

But he wasn't in the mood to be playful. "If I do it, I'll rip something."

Her eyes widened a bit, but she looked as if the idea pleased her.

He started unbuttoning his shirt. It was as if they were in a race to see who could undress first. Soon their clothes littered the bed and the floor, and then he was beside her, taking her into his arms, kissing her as if it were the last kiss they'd ever share.

April raked her nails down his back and he liked the idea of her scratches on him. If this was going to be a mating ritual, he wanted them both to be branded with it, to never forget it, to be able to relive it in their minds and go there because thinking about it was exciting. The desire he felt tonight didn't want to be confined or restrained, and he let it free because he wanted April to match it.

She didn't disappoint him. She seemed as greedy to give him pleasure as he was to give her pleasure. He kissed her neck. In turn, she nipped his chest. She reached for him, taking him in her hands. Desire between them that had seemed to build up for years erupted. Although yesterday she'd said her leg was fine, when he ran his hands over her body, he was mindful of it and her fall. Desire could stamp out pain. The need for climax could send magical feelings through the rest of the body. That's what had happened the last two nights. But now she moved as if she'd never fallen. She bent her legs and cradled him between her thighs. He thrust into her, meaning to forget everything in the attic, everything in the past, everything that meant nothing in this moment.

Their passion went wild. Their bodies reached the melting point together. When April cried her release, Gabe was right with her, experiencing ecstasy of his own.

Afterward, he collapsed beside her and held her tightly.

But he came back to earth with a jolt when April murmured, "We didn't use protection."

No, they hadn't. Neither of them had been thinking clearly enough to be smart.

The way April's body was tucked into his, seemingly relaxed, he suspected little sleep the past two nights had caught up with her.

He brushed her hair over her shoulder and whispered next to her ear, "We'll talk about it in the morning."

She must have agreed with him because she snuggled deeper into him, nodded, and sighed.

Although tonight April had fallen asleep almost as easily as Stephie, Gabe couldn't find slumber. What if April *did* get pregnant? What if she didn't want to join their lives? What if she ran off as she had five years ago? Had she left because of her career? Or had she left because a relationship had scared her? Was he ready to jump back in to something serious? A commitment with promises as he'd made once before?

Those receipts in the attic gnawed at him. The open box seemed to beckon to him.

He extricated himself from April, lifted his jeans from the edge of the bed, and put them on. He took a last look at her before he left the room. On her side, her hair splayed across one of his pillows, he liked the picture of her there.

His feet and chest bare, he went up to the attic, intent on finishing what he'd started. He was still hot from what he and April had done, so the cooler temperature felt good on his skin. Crossing to the box, he sat on the floor once more. He lifted the receipts he'd examined before and nothing had changed. He'd never noticed expenses like this. He'd never monitored Vanessa's check writing or how much she spent. She contributed to some of their house expenses but for the most part, her salary was hers.

He found a brochure from one of the accounts she worked with. He even found a candy wrapper. She'd had a penchant for peanuts and caramel, and he'd often teased her about it. At the beginning anyway.

He lifted out about ten sheets of paper that were folded together. A green plastic clip made sure they didn't separate. Now he slipped off the clip and unfolded the papers. They were e-mails. E-mails from Larry Powell.

Chapter Nine

Gabe shifted through the e-mails, one by one. Unable to comprehend what he was seeing, what struck him most vividly at first was the span. They stretched over a three-year period, from almost a year before Stephie was born until the night of Vanessa's accident. Vanessa and Larry Powell's accident.

Gabe didn't know how he'd been so blind, how he'd had such tunnel vision, how he hadn't noticed his wife was having an affair under his nose. He felt like a complete fool. He'd thought promises the day they'd wed meant something. He'd expected fidelity to be a value they both embraced. He believed their marriage had been important to them both. How could Vanessa have hidden so much so well?

The e-mails began with a flirty tone. They must have sent them back and forth at work. *Meet me for a drink after work?* Larry Powell asked. *I can make you happier than any Cosmopolitan for Happy Hour.* Larry's next e-mail had Vanessa's reply, a one-liner that read, *That sounds exciting.*

She'd wanted excitement.

Gabe had wanted a family.

Larry's follow-up e-mail had been a one-liner. *Excitement is my middle name. Meet me at Rafferty's.*

Gabe knew the pub was located not far from where Vanessa had worked.

Why had she kept these? For the same reason any woman kept love letters?

But these e-mails weren't about love. Gabe didn't want to read them, he really didn't. Yet he was fascinated by them in a horrified way. Besides logistics, meeting places, and dates, and times there were sexual references and playful banter about what they wanted to do to each other when they were alone.

However, after that, came the more serious e-mails. Vanessa had written—*I'm pregnant. What are we going to do?* She'd known who Stephie belonged to right from the start. And then… Larry's reply was succinct. *Have sex with your husband so he believes the baby's his. Have lots of it.*

Gabe remembered that time. He remembered when Vanessa had been amorous, and he'd felt that somehow they'd renewed their commitment to each other. How *stupid* he'd been. She'd just been laying the groundwork. Stephie hadn't been three weeks premature. At seven pounds, she'd been her perfect weight and right on time.

What kind of woman had Vanessa been?

What kind of man had Larry Powell been?

But that answer was soon evident enough in one of the last e-mails. Vanessa had written—*I can't live a lie. I have to tell Gabe.* But Larry had written back—*Don't be foolish. I'm not daddy material. I don't want the responsibility of a kid and you know it. We're fun and games, Vanessa, not picket fences and castles in the air.*

Had Vanessa and Larry argued the night of the accident? Had an argument caused the accident?

One thought played in Gabe's head above all the rest. *Stephie's not my daughter.*

Yet as soon as he had the thought, memories contradicted it. He'd fed her as a newborn. He'd changed diapers in the middle of the night. He'd witnessed her first smile and her first step. He'd rocked her when she'd had bad dreams. He'd given her unconditional love that he hadn't even known existed before she was born. She was *his* daughter, no matter what any scientific test said.

He sat there for a long while, examining his marriage to Vanessa with a fine-tooth comb. Apparently there were more flaws than he'd ever imagined. What had she told him the night of the accident? "I can't get out of this meeting. I have a complicated problem to deal with. I might be late getting home."

Had her eyes looked a little haunted that night? Why? Because she was going to try to convince Larry Powell they should be together? When she knew deep down in her heart that wasn't what he wanted? Or because she knew in the long run, she was going to have to hurt Gabe irrevocably?

He remembered the police officer coming to his door. He remembered calling April, bundling up Stephie, meeting April at the hospital. She'd watched Stephie while he'd gone in with Vanessa, and then he'd taken Stephie so she could sit with her sister. One of the nurses had said she was on a break and could watch Stephie if he wanted to go in, too. He'd overheard April whisper, "I promise" to her sister.

What had she promised Vanessa? At the time, he'd thought she'd promised to watch over Stephie. But what if she'd promised something else? What if she knew?

That thought drove him to his feet. It caused him to throw the e-mails into the box and charge down the stairs.

April must have heard his feet pounding in the hall because she was already sitting up in the bed when he rushed into the room.

"What's wrong?" she asked groggily.

He studied her for a long moment before he answered, hardening his heart, erecting those walls around it again for self-preservation.

"Stephie's not my daughter."

To his dismay, he didn't see surprise in her eyes. In fact, he saw resignation. When April was silent, Gabe accused her of her lie of omission. "You knew, didn't you?"

She looked shaken now as if she didn't know what to do, as if she didn't know whether she should get out of bed and get dressed, cover up with a sheet, go to him, or stay where she was. She covered with the sheet. "Not all along. The night of the accident, Vanessa confided in me."

"I'm supposed to believe *you*, her sister, didn't know about the affair she was having behind my back? I have all the e-mails to document it."

"Vanessa and I were close once, but after the two of you married, we weren't. I didn't know about the affair, Gabe. Honest, I didn't."

"So what exactly did she tell you?" He wanted to know it all now, the whole truth and nothing but.

April looked as if she'd rather be any place else but in his bed, and he certainly understood that. But he wasn't going to make her feel better, not when his world had just come apart at the seams.

Apparently she recognized his dogged determination to ferret out every detail because she said in a low voice, "Vanessa knew she was dying. She knew she wasn't going to make it. She made me promise so many things. The first was, of course, to take care of Stephie...to help *you* take care of Stephie."

If he felt any softening toward Vanessa at all, it was over this point. "What else?" he demanded to know.

April looked haunted. "She told me the whole story before she died." She hesitated, then went on. "After Stephie was born, she wasn't sure if you were the father."

He and Vanessa had had a sex life, though it obviously wasn't anything like she'd enjoyed with Larry Powell.

"And then?" Gabe prodded.

"She told me that about a month before the night of the accident, she had a DNA test done. Larry wanted to know for sure."

"And the results came back that with all likelihood, he was Stephie's dad."

"The test determined he was her biological father, Gabe, not her real father. Don't you see that?"

His heart felt as if it were ripping in two. "No. What I see is a woman who lied to me over and over again. Do you know what happened the night she died?"

Now April did reach for her clothes. Hurriedly, she pulled her sweater over her head, forgetting about the bra that lay on the floor. She stepped into her panties, pulled on her jeans, and stood before him, looking bedraggled, miserable, and upset.

"Why is this necessary, Gabe? Why do you have to know every detail?"

"Because I do."

She took a deep breath, avoided looking at his naked chest, at his mouth, and kept her gaze on his.

"Vanessa and Larry were arguing when they had the accident. Larry wanted things to stay the same. She wanted to give you custody of Stephie, ask for a divorce, and run off with him."

Gabe thought he actually might stop breathing. *This* was the woman he'd married? *This* was the woman he'd thought he loved? He asked in a gravelly voice, "She was willing to toss away Stephie as if she didn't matter?"

April was already shaking her head. "No. She knew how much you loved Stephie. She felt you were a good dad. Actually, I don't think she felt fit to be a mother. It was a solution, but one Larry didn't want any part of."

Gabe could hardly wrap his mind around it.

"You said she made you make promises. What other promises besides watching over Stephie?" But before he asked, he suspected he already knew the answer.

"She wanted me to keep it all a secret. She didn't want your feelings for Stephie to ever change. Gabe, I've been torn apart by this, not knowing the right thing to do. Of course, I made those promises that night. That's what she needed to hear. But afterward…but afterward, I didn't know what was worse—you living a lie or you finding out Stephie wasn't your daughter and feeling differently about her. I was trying to protect you and your relationship with Stephie. It wasn't about Vanessa at all any more. But then, after you and I…" She trailed off. "After you and I made love, I knew I had to tell you the truth. I've been trying to figure out how to do it. I was going to tell you tonight. But then Mother called, and when I got home…" She stopped. "You wanted me."

Yes, he had. But other emotions were overtaking his desire for her. "You betrayed me. You should have told me. You didn't trust me to love Stephie enough to cherish her, to always act as her father, whether it was a biological fact or not. You know what that means? That means you didn't trust me now any more than you did five years ago. That means if we don't have trust, we have *nothing* between us."

"You can't deny what we have between us," she protested, her voice trembling. "Look what happened tonight. Unless…" She stopped and put her hand over her mouth. Her gaze searched his and then she shakily asked, "Unless…what did you find in that box in the attic before I came home?"

He felt uncomfortable with that question and

wasn't sure why. "Nothing specific. I just found some receipts. She'd bought a couple of men's things, things I never received. I thought maybe she'd purchased them for work."

Now April's eyes accused *him*. "Did you, Gabe? Or deep down did you know about this? Did you guess what she had done?" April took a step back away from him. "Did you have all that desire for me tonight to get back at Vanessa? Did you come on to me like that because you wanted me to be hungry for you in a way Vanessa never was? Is that what the past few days have been all about?"

He felt himself go as pale as April, yet he couldn't accept what she was saying had driven him into bed with her. So he went on the defensive. "You kept a secret you had no right to keep. You made a promise that you knew would hurt everyone in the long run."

"I made a promise to watch over Stephie, and I've kept it," she reminded him, her voice rising.

"You've chosen a hell of a way to watch over her, and I have to wonder if I hadn't found those e-mails upstairs, if you would *ever* have told me."

Tears came to April's eyes now, and he hardened himself against them.

She said, "You're not going to believe anything I

say now, are you?"

"No."

That word was like a cannonball hitting the wall. The reverberation ended in a silence that was dark and almost suffocating.

He could see that as April picked up her socks and her sneakers. He could feel it as she went to the door, turned around, and said, "I'm going to stay in a motel tonight. Tomorrow, I'll figure out what to do next. But no matter what you think of me, Gabe, no matter what you think about Vanessa, Stephie is your daughter in every way that matters."

After April left his room, Gabe closed the door. Then he sat on the bed and dropped his head into his hands.

****

The following day, April knew she had to get out of the motel room bed or she'd stay there forever. Desolate last night when she'd left Gabe, she'd checked into this motel, not really caring where she was or what she was doing. She'd sat for hours in the dark in her room, thinking, trying to figure out what she could have done differently. Hurting Gabe had been the only option, and she hadn't wanted to hurt him. Maybe she hadn't trusted him as much as she should have where Stephie was concerned. Maybe she should have trusted his feelings for Stephie wouldn't change. But she'd been afraid to take that chance.

That had been the problem. She'd been afraid too much all along with anything that concerned Gabe.

Not knowing what else to do, she called her mother. If ever there was a time she needed her—

Winnifred answered her cell phone with, "It's barely nine o'clock."

April hadn't even known what time it was. She just knew the sun was up, she'd been lying there too long, and she had to do *something*.

"I need to see you," April said.

"April, what's wrong? I haven't had my first morning coffee. I can douse some cold water on my face if you need me to."

"Stephie isn't Gabe's daughter."

There was stark silence, and April guessed that surprise had awakened her mother more than any splash of cold water.

"Oh my." Somehow, her mother put a whole world of feeling in those two words. "Where are you?"

"I'm in a motel."

"That's ridiculous. I'll ask Clarice if you can come stay here."

"I'm fine here, Mother. I just need to figure out what to do next. Gabe hates me. We were getting close and then he found papers in the attic, and now…he hates me."

"I doubt that very much," Winnifred said. "Oh, you might think he does. *He* might think he does. Tell me what happened."

So April did.

"Vanessa needed to confess and you were her confessor. Of course, you had to keep her secret."

"There's no 'of course' about it. And Gabe certainly doesn't see it that way."

"Give him a little time. You and Vanessa were sisters, for goodness sake. That's a bond that can't be broken, even over lost love."

April kept silent.

"Don't think I didn't know you still loved Gabe when you left. A mother knows these things. But you weren't ready for what he had to offer, and nothing I said could have stopped you."

That was probably true.

"Honey, I was a poor example for both you and Vanessa. Sure, what Vanessa did was awful and mostly her fault. But if she had seen better at home, maybe she would have done better."

"I could never do that to anyone."

"That's you." Winnifred sighed. "Your sister put you in an untenable situation."

"Gabe will never forgive me."

"*Never* is a long time, April. Why don't you come over here? We'll have tea and try to figure out what we can do about this."

There was nothing else April could do right now, so she agreed. "I'll be there in about half an hour."

****

Nicholas never called before he came over, and Gabe supposed that was probably a good thing because he would have told him not to come.

Unable to concentrate on anything except what had happened last night, Gabe hadn't gone into work today. Unlike yesterday, Stephie had been quiet, almost apathetic. Gabe attributed that to April being gone because Stephie missed her already.

He wasn't going there.

Nicholas took one look at Gabe and said, "I should have brought my best bottle of brandy. I thought we could play basketball."

"I can't."

Nicholas looked around, saw Stephie in the living room watching a DVD.

"Is April not here?"

"April left." There must have been a little too much vehemence in that last word because Nicholas arched his brows.

"Left to go back to Boston?"

"I don't know."

"Shake it loose, Gabe, because you're not making sense. Tell me what's going on."

So after a lowered voice and saying, "Stephie's not my daughter…I found e-mails…April knew it all along," Nicholas got the gist of exactly what was happening.

He went to the counter, poured himself a cup of coffee from the second pot Gabe had brewed that day, poured another mug for Gabe and took them both to the table. Then he pointed to the chair. Both of them sat and Gabe just turned the mug around and around, staring into it, unable to find any answers.

Nicholas blew on his coffee, sipped it, and set down the mug. "You do see, don't you, that April was caught in a trap?"

"No, I don't. She could have told me."

"Let's see. When would have been a good time to tell you? Right after Vanessa died? Those first months when you were a grieving husband?"

"I wouldn't have been a grieving husband if I had known what had happened."

"That's bull. I don't know exactly how much you felt for Vanessa, but you felt something, and you would have grieved. When someone dies, no matter what they've done, you still miss them."

When Gabe didn't respond, Nicholas went on. "Or maybe April should have told you when she was home for Stephie's birthday party, or maybe when you were having a hard time finding someone to watch her, or maybe—"

"I get it. No time was good, and that's the point. She should have just told me."

"And if she had, would you have lumped her in the same category as Vanessa? After all, Vanessa confided in *her*, not you. You know, from what you tell me, for once in her life, maybe Vanessa was being selfless. Maybe Vanessa was actually thinking about what was best for her daughter."

"She was ready to give her up."

"Maybe because she thought Stephie would have a

better life if she did, a better life with *you*. She wanted you to be Stephie's dad, no matter what *she* wanted, or who she wanted to be with."

Gabe just shook his head. "Don't weave this into something it isn't."

"I'm trying to give your dead wife the benefit of the doubt. Maybe you should do the same. Maybe you should give April the benefit of the doubt."

"April should have told me," he said again. "When we—"

"When you what?" Nicholas asked, but his tone said he might already know.

"We got closer again."

"You had sex."

Gabe inhaled deeply and exhaled it just as deeply.

All of a sudden, he heard crying coming from the living room. That crying he knew. It wasn't on the DVD. Standing, he went to the sofa and saw Stephie curled in a ball, tears running down her cheeks.

"What's wrong, baby?"

He almost expected her to say "I miss April", but she didn't. She said, "I hurt all over, Daddy."

Fear like nothing he'd ever experienced lanced through Gabe. He felt her forehead and it was hot, much too hot.

"I have to call the doctor," he said, plucking his phone from his belt.

"You might want to take her temperature first," Nicholas said practically, "Especially if you want a doctor to help."

"That hurting all over. I've heard about kids coming down with meningitis. She could have that. She could have—"

"Gabe, get a grip. Where's the thermometer? I'll get it."

"In the upstairs bathroom. The drawer in the vanity." He took Stephie into his arms and held her. Nothing could happen to his little girl. Nothing. He wouldn't let it. He'd protect her until he couldn't any longer, and then he'd find somebody else who could.

Chapter Ten

A tech escorted April to a cubicle in the ER. Nicholas had called her to tell her what was happening. Not Gabe. And Gabe didn't know Nicholas had called her. What a mess.

At first she'd wondered if she should come, but her instincts told her she should. Her love for Stephie told her she should. Her mother and Nicholas told her she should.

At the doorway to the room, she stopped. Stephie looked so small lying in the bed, her blond hair spread on the pillow, her eyes closed. She was hooked up to an IV and a monitor. Gabe was sitting by her bedside, his large hands holding one of her little ones.

"How is she?" April asked softly, only stepping a

few paces into the room.

Gabe raised his head and his gaze met hers. "She has a strep infection. They're pumping fluids and antibiotics into her, and I think they're going to keep her overnight."

"Do you mind if I come in?"

He didn't look as if he wanted her there. Also, he looked as if he needed a hug. But she knew she couldn't touch him. She knew he wouldn't let her touch him.

Going to the other side of the bed, April pulled a chair up to it and sat. After stroking Stephie's hair back from her brow, she kissed her on the cheek.

"They let me come back when I told them I was her aunt," she said.

Gabe and April didn't speak as they sat there watching Stephie. April didn't know if they'd ever really talk again, but she knew she had to try. She'd gone over everything and searched the depths of her soul. Whether Gabe wanted to listen to her or not, she had to say what was in her heart.

When Gabe leaned away from the bed and rubbed the back of his neck, she asked, "Can we step out to the hall for a few minutes?"

"April, this isn't the time or the place for a long

discussion."

"It won't be a long discussion. I just need to tell you something."

He looked reluctant to leave his daughter, or maybe just reluctant to talk to her. But he stepped outside the cubicle with her into the hall.

Reluctant to begin, she knew she must. "I should have trusted you and your feelings for Stephie. I want you to also understand when I make a promise, I don't do it lightly. I know it can be a sacred thing. Keeping my promise to Vanessa was important, but I was afraid keeping it would hurt you. I didn't want to do that, Gabe, not under any circumstances."

When Gabe didn't look moved, she realized she had to be absolutely honest with him. "Five years ago, I left because I was scared. I was in love with you and didn't know how to *be* in love. So I ran. But I do love you, Gabe. I want to show you how much I love you and that I can trust you if you give me the chance. But if you can't, I'll understand and go back to Boston."

The nerve in Gabe's jaw worked but he didn't speak.

April knew she was only causing him more heartache by being here. So she said, "I'll let you sit with Stephie. If you need me, I'm just a phone call away."

Then she started down the hall to the reception area.

****

Gabe watched April walk away for about a minute.

A nurse came bustling in to Stephie's cubicle and he told her, "I'll be right back."

As he'd been sitting by Stephie's bedside, everything Nicholas had said had begun to make sense. He loved his daughter and always would. Nothing would ever change that. She was his and would always be.

Sitting there, waiting for the doctor to tell him what was wrong with her, he'd prayed. But he hadn't prayed just for Stephie. He'd prayed that he'd know what to do.

As soon as he'd seen April walk away, he'd realized what he had to do. He had to make everything right between them. He had to forgive her, and maybe not even that. Had she really done anything wrong?

Going over her words, feeling her turmoil, he realized she hadn't. Putting himself in her position, he wasn't sure what he would have done in her place, and he had to tell her that. He had to tell her that, and a heck of a lot more.

She'd reached the outside portico when he came up behind her and grabbed her arm. "April. Don't go."

"Gabe."

He pulled her to the side where the lights weren't quite as glaring. When she looked up at him, he saw hope in her eyes and that gave *him* hope that maybe they could have a future.

"I never should have married Vanessa," he admitted. "I did us both a disservice. I did a lot of thinking today. Yes, I was committed to her and our marriage. But, somehow, I wonder if she sensed I still had feelings for you. I hadn't even admitted that to myself. Five years ago I should have asked you to stay. I should have faced your fears with you. I'm not going to let you walk out of my life again. I love you April Remmington. Can you forgive me for my self-righteous attitude? For seeing a wrong you didn't commit? I'm as much to blame as anyone else in everything that's happened. Will you give me a second chance to love you for the rest of our lives?"

There was a moment of shocked surprise when his

heart almost dropped to the pavement, but then she was reaching for him, wrapping her arms around him, joyfully holding him.

"I love you, Gabe. I'll love you forever."

Forever was more than he could have ever wished for. Forever was how he felt about her.

After a long deep kiss, he wrapped his arm around her, and they walked back into the hospital…to the daughter who would belong to them both.

Epilogue

Two days before Christmas, April crouched down with Stephie in the nave of the church. "You look perfect," she said, adjusting the little collar on Stephie's red velvet dress. "Remember everything we practiced?"

Stephie nodded, the red ribbons in her hair bobbing as she did. The basket she carried was filled with red rose petals, and she was going to scatter them in front of April as April walked down the aisle.

"Daddy says I don't have to throw them far."

"Your daddy's right."

"Daddy said you're the best gift we could get for Christmas, and you know what?"

April felt her eyes tearing up. "What?"

"In that dress, you look like the angel on our Christmas tree."

April laughed. The white taffeta creation with seed pearls was princess-like, and she loved it. It was perfect for tonight, and she hoped Gabe thought so too. She glanced up at the altar where Nicholas stood beside her husband-to-be.

Her mother tapped her on the shoulder. Doing double duty, her mother was going to walk her down the aisle, as well as act as Matron of Honor. In a green two-piece suit with an ankle-length skirt, she was stunning. Her mom was indeed moving back to Cedar Corners, and to everyone's surprise, her new beau had decided to retire and do the same. He was sitting in the front pew. The way he looked at her mother, April thought her mom might change her mind about marriage.

The music began to play. After a last hug for Stephie, April straightened, held her head high, and took her mother's hand.

The walk down the aisle seemed endless but she recognized many of Gabe's friends that she was coming to know as well as his employees. She had quit her job in Boston and gone to work for Nicholas' firm. The transition hadn't seemed like a transition at all. Maybe that was the way it should be when life was right.

And this was right.

Stephie's rose petals decided each of April's footsteps as she moved forward toward a life she'd dreamed of. Sure there would be adjustments, but one thing was certain. She loved Gabe and he loved her.

At the front of the church, Winnifred kissed April's cheek, took her bouquet, and Stephie's hand.

April faced Gabe and he whispered, "You look beautiful."

"You look like a groom," she said, trying to keep the tears at bay.

He took her hand and squeezed it, telling her he understood. The minister welcomed everyone, spoke a few moments about marriage, and then said, "The bride and groom have written their own vows." He nodded to April.

"I, April Remmington, promise to love you, no matter what. I promise to be vulnerable and honest, sharing my life, my heart and my soul with you. I will cherish each and every day we have together, and every moment I spend with Stephie, too. I hope I can be the mom she needs…the wife you need. I promise you that every day, that's what I'll strive for. Whether we have a rocky road, a smooth road, or an unpaved road, I promise I will hold your hand and never let go. I will trust you, believe in you, respect you, and tell you how much I love you until my dying day."

She could see her words had moved Gabe, and now he took both of her hands and squeezed hard.

"I know promises are important to both of us," he said with resounding certainty. "I know I can believe yours, and you can believe mine. I promise you that today is only the beginning. You are a part of me, April, a part I never thought I'd find. You're that missing piece that gives me peace, and makes my life more worthwhile. I want you to be Stephie's mother in every sense of the word, just as I am her dad. Together we'll raise her with values and optimism, with the cheekiness she'll need to fight the world. I know we can do that together. I promise you all my love, my fidelity, my strength, and my protection. I will support your aspirations and help you make your decisions. I will be beside you whenever you need me. I love you, April, and this will be the best Christmas I ever had, because I have the gift of your love. I give you the gift of mine."

April was openly crying now. She just couldn't help it. But they were joyful tears and she was sure

Gabe knew that. They sealed their vows by giving each other rings, bands of gold that would encircle them for a lifetime.

At the end of the ceremony, the minister blessed them and announced clearly, "I present to you April and Gabe Chronister, husband and wife."

"You can kiss her now," he said to Gabe.

Gabe did to a breakout of applause from all the guests in the pews.

As he lifted his head, he whispered to April, "Winnifred's taking Stephie to her place to wrap presents all day tomorrow, so we'll have a whole day for a honeymoon."

"And the rest of our lives," April returned easily.

Gabe took her in his arms and kissed her again.

BIOGRAPHY
Karen Rose Smith

Award-winning author Karen Rose Smith was born in Pennsylvania. Although she was an only child, she remembers the bonds of an extended family. Since her father came from a family of ten and her mother, a family of seven, there were always aunts, uncles and cousins visiting on weekends. Family is a strong theme in her books and she suspects her childhood memories are the reason.

In college, Karen began writing poetry and also met her husband to be. They both began married life as teachers, but when their son was born, Karen decided to try her hand at a home-decorating business. She returned to teaching for a while but changes in her life led her to writing romance fiction. Now she writes romances and mysteries full time. She has sold over 80 novels since 1991.

Presently, she is hard at work on a series for Harlequin Special Edition as well as the Caprice De Luca home stager mystery series for Kensington Books. When she isn't writing, she cares for three rescue cats, gardens, and cooks. Married to her college sweetheart since 1971, believing in the power of love and commitment, she envisions herself writing relationship novels, both romance and mystery, for a long time to come!

KAREN ROSE SMITH BOOKS AVAILABLE IN E-BOOK FORMAT

FOREVER LOVE Series
April's Promise

FINDING MR. RIGHT Series
Kit and Kisses, Book 1
Forever After, Book 2
When Mom Meets Dad, Book 3 *
Falling For Her Boss, Book 4 *
Toys and Baby Wishes, Book 5 *
Love in Bloom, Book 6
Ribbons and Rainbows, Book 7 *
Wish on the Moon, Book 8 *
A Man Worth Loving, Book 9 *

SEARCH FOR LOVE Series
Nathan's Vow, Book 1 *
Jake's Bride, Book 2 *
Always Devoted, Book 3 *
Always Her Cowboy, Book 4 *
Heartfire, Book 5

Cassidy's Cowboy, Book 6 *
Her Sister, Book 7 *

EVERYDAY LOVE Short Story Series
Everyday Cinderellas, Vol. 1
Everyday Prince Charming, Vol. 2
Everyday Romance, Vol.3

Garden of Fantasy
Abigail and Mistletoe
Writing is a Business

SCIENCE FICTION SHORT STORY COLLECTION
Journey Into Chaos

BOXED SETS
Finding Mr. Right Box Set One
Finding Mr. Right Boxed Set Two
Search For Love Boxed Set One
Search For Love Boxed Set Two
Everyday Love Boxed Set

* Also available in audio book format

Excerpt from HER SISTER
Search For Love series, Book 7

Prologue

Where is Lynnie? Where did she go?

In her mind, five-year-old Clare Thaddeus called to her little sister—*Come back, Lynnie. Please come back.*

The huge policeman crouched down in front of Clare's mother at the sofa and said in a deep, slow voice, "Mrs. Thaddeus, I know you're terribly upset. But I need details. We've got an hour before daylight. If your daughter wandered outside—"

Clare's father, who'd been talking to another man in blue, glanced at her, and Clare huddled down deeper into the big green armchair. Her dad didn't come to her but rather went to her mom, sank down beside her and wrapped his arm around her. Then he spoke to the officer. "Our daughter, Lynnie, is three. She would never go outside into the dark on her own."

"Tell us again where you were last night," the

policeman demanded in a not-so-nice voice.

"I worked late, preparing a brief."

"Until five a.m.?"

"Yes, until five a.m. As I told you, I always check the girls' rooms before turning in. Lynnie wasn't in her bed. I woke my wife. We looked through the whole house and then we called you."

Clare had been sleeping in her brand new room. They'd moved in here—she studied her hand and counted her fingers—five days ago. Boxes were still stacked down here and upstairs. The house was okay. There were more rooms for her and Lynnie to play hide and seek. But she didn't like being alone in her own room at night. She'd liked it better when she and Lynnie had slept in the same room.

Earlier she'd thought she'd heard Lynnie's door open…thought her sister was going to the bathroom and might come in and crawl into bed with her. But she'd been *so* sleepy. She and Lynnie had been running through the hose sprayer all afternoon in the backyard while Mommy unpacked. She was supposed to watch her sister. She was always supposed to look out for Lynnie. That's what big sisters did.

Where had Lynnie gone?

Then Clare remembered the blue car that had

driven down the alley in back of the yard lots of times. The man had stopped once and watched them. But she'd thought he might be one of their new neighbors who just wanted to say hi.

Should she tell the policeman?

He was so big, and he looked mad. Her dad looked mad, too, as he asked, "Why do you want to question me and my wife separately?"

"That's just the way we do it, Mr. Thaddeus."

Although she was scared of the two big men in blue uniforms, she knew her mommy and daddy wouldn't let them hurt her. Policemen helped, didn't they? They were going to help find Lynnie.

She slipped off of the chair, went over to the sofa and tugged on her mother's arm. "Mommy, when I was playing—"

The doorbell rang.

"Are you expecting someone?" the policeman asked, his brows arched.

Not sounding at all like herself, her mother answered, "I called a friend."

"Before or after you called us?"

Her mother's face turned red. "*After*, of course."

"Mommy." She tugged on her mother's arm again while one of the policemen went to the door.

Her mother took Clare's hand. "Not now, honey. Natalie's going to take care of you for a little while so we can talk to the officers."

"But, Mommy—"

Her mom's best friend, Natalie Barlow, rushed into the living room looking as upset as her mom and dad. "What can I do?"

Her father answered quickly. "Can you take Clare upstairs? And can you call our old neighbors? Maybe they'll help search. I've got to get out there looking, but I have to finish answering questions first."

Natalie gave Clare a weak smile and took her hand. "Come on, honey. Let's go upstairs for a while."

Her mom kissed her.

Her dad gave her a nod.

She tried again. "When I was playing with Lynnie—"

Tears fell down her mom's cheeks. Her dad said, "Not now. Go upstairs with Natalie."

What she had to say wasn't important. The man in the blue car didn't matter. Only Lynnie mattered.

As Clare followed Natalie upstairs, she got very afraid. What if the policemen couldn't find Lynnie? Is that why her mommy was crying? Because she didn't think they could? Was that why her dad was mad?

Natalie bent down to her. "I don't want you to worry. Everything's going to be all right."

But Clare knew better. If Lynnie didn't come home, nothing would ever be right again.

Chapter One

"I'm not taking it back. I bought it with my own money." Shara Thaddeus stared at her mother defiantly, standing her ground. At sixteen, she was Clare's payback for the trouble Clare had given her parents when <u>she</u> was sixteen, though certainly not for the same reason.

At thirty-two and a single parent, Clare didn't know what to do with Shara any more than her parents had known what to do with her. She'd rebelled because she'd wanted their attention. *Any* of their attention. All of their attention. When Lynnie had been around, Clare had loved her and protected her and been her big sister. But after she'd disappeared, it was as if Clare hadn't existed.

Everything was always about Lynnie. And Clare had just wanted her parents to realize that although her sister was gone, *she* was still there.

Shara, on the other hand, had always had all of Clare's attention. What she didn't have was a father. She'd been a precocious child, constantly testing her boundaries. Sometimes Clare just got weary of being a watchdog. But yet wasn't that what parents were supposed to do?

After taking a deep breath for patience then putting her chin-length brown hair behind her ears, she reached out and took the blouse from Shara's hands. It really wasn't a blouse, just a stretch lace concoction that *her* daughter wasn't going to be caught dead in. "If you wear this out on the street, you'll get arrested. What did you buy to go with it?" She meant to keep her tone curious but it sounded judgmental anyway.

Shara produced a pair of black leather shorts that Clare suspected would fit too snugly.

"The outfit goes back. It's not appropriate for school. It's not appropriate to wear to the mall. It's not appropriate to be caught dusting the house in. What were you thinking?"

"I'm thinking there are a few boys who would

think I'm hot."

Counting to ten had never been a strategy that worked well for Clare, especially when her daughter was deliberately trying to push her buttons. But she tried it again, nonetheless, not meeting with any more success than she'd achieved the last time. She prayed for patience, or wisdom or anything that would help deal with her daughter.

Finally, in a friendly tone she asked, "Care to give me their names? Maybe I can do background checks."

Shara studied her mother, trying to decide if she was joking or serious. "Brad said he likes me in black."

"Brad doesn't need to like you in anything. He's a senior. You're a sophomore. We've talked about this, Shara. He has a reputation and I don't want him giving *you* a reputation."

"You are wound *so* tight," Shara mumbled.

Before Clare could deal with *that* assessment, the telephone rang. She glanced at it, thought about letting it ring, letting the answering machine take over. But maybe both she and her daughter needed a few minutes to cool down. She saw from the Caller ID that it was her mom's home number. This would probably be a short conversation. They never had much to say to each other.

Clare watched Shara take the new outfit and her other bags to her room. "They go back," Clare called after her.

Her daughter didn't bother to reply.

Clare greeted her mom with a chipper "hello," wondering what she was going to put together for supper. As an X-ray technician at the hospital, she usually arrived home after Shara. Today, however, Shara had asked her if she could stop at the mall for an hour or so after school and Clare had agreed. It looked as if they'd both be taking a trip after supper to return Shara's purchases. Maybe they should just leave now and grab pizza there. The mall on an October Friday night would be busy.

"Clare?"

The tiny crack in her mother's voice made Clare pull in a breath. "What's wrong? Has something happened to Dad?"

Although her father and mother had divorced two years after Lynnie had disappeared, Clare had desperately tried to hold onto bonds with both of them.

"I haven't heard from your father in weeks. The last time I saw him was at the picnic you had Labor

Day weekend."

It was really strange. Her parents had once had a good marriage until Lynnie was taken. Now they were awkward together whenever they had to be in the same room. Clare always felt as if she were the cause of that awkwardness, always felt as if she should do something to make it all better, always felt as if she was the neutral territory in the middle of a decades-old war.

After a short pause, her mother explained, "Detective Grove called me. He already spoke to your father."

Clare's heart skipped a beat. "Detective Grove?" The picture of a tall lean man in a rumpled suit flashed in her mind—the man who had taken over Lynnie's investigation after the patrol officers' first visit.

"Do you remember him?" her mother asked gently—too gently—and Clare had a shivery premonition of what could be coming.

"Didn't he retire?" she asked her mom, her heart racing now.

"Yes, he did. But he's not really keen on retirement and he's been…working a few cold cases." Her mother's voice was edgier than usual and a little wobbly, too.

"What are you trying to tell me, Mom?" Clare's hands became sweaty as she thought about all the possibilities. Lynnie's face at three and a half was still so vivid in her mind—the face they'd used on posters...the face she'd envisioned floating in a river...the face on the body in nightmares that had been buried in a ditch. The *not* knowing had always been worse than knowing. The <u>not</u> knowing is what had torn them all apart. Clare really believed that if the police had found Lynnie's body somewhere, maybe they could have gone on as a family.

Maybe.

"He wants to meet with us tomorrow morning. You, me and your dad. He thinks he has a lead."

Clare's throat went desert dry. Even though she'd only been five, she remembered the hope that had filled her parents' faces whenever a new lead had been phoned in, whenever the police had gotten a tip from an informer on the street, whenever there was a chance that Lynnie might have been spotted. She also remembered the expression on their faces when all those hopes had been dashed and one day had turned into the next without teaching them anything new.

Except that they were losing each other, hour by

hour, day by day, week by week.

"What kind of lead?" Clare asked, trying to control the shakiness in her voice.

"He wouldn't tell me over the phone. He's working out of his home, so I offered the use of my office at *Yesteryear*. Can you be there tomorrow at ten?"

Her father wouldn't like meeting at her mother's shop. Now and then he'd complained to Clare that her mother was lost in the past. He didn't like the mustiness of the store or what the old furniture represented—a history that couldn't be changed…a child who would never come home. Her mother didn't see it that way at all. Her mother liked to relive every memory she had. She wrapped herself in the reminiscence of what she told Clare were the happiest years of her life. More than that, *Yesteryear* had given her a reason to get up each day, a reason to search for old furniture if not for her daughter, though Clare suspected she still looked for Lynnie everywhere she went.

Trying to prepare herself for the meeting, she shored up her courage and asked, "Did Detective Grove say whether this lead means Lynnie's alive or dead?"

A sharp intake of breath met her question and then her mom answered, "He didn't say, and I didn't ask. I still have hope, Clare. I always have."

Yes, her mother had held onto the hope that Lynnie was still alive, that some misguided woman had taken her and raised her for her own. But a misguided woman didn't steal a child from someone's house in the middle of the night.

False hope was worse than no hope at all. Clare and her dad understood each other on that one point, at least.

"I'll be there tomorrow, Mom, but please don't—" She wasn't sure how to say it.

"Please don't believe in the best rather than the worst? Oh, Clare. Maybe as you get older you'll learn that believing in the best is the only way to get through some days. I'll see you in the morning, honey."

Clare and her mother weren't on the same wavelength…would never be on the same wavelength. Just like her and Shara?

She said goodbye, hung up the phone and went to her daughter's room. Arguing with Shara would postpone thinking about the meeting tomorrow morning…a meeting that could shake up all of their lives once more.